Shivshakti

The Continuous Continuum

ANITA RAJANI

Copyright © 2021 by **Anita Rajani**
All rights reserved. This book or any portion thereof may not be reproduced or used in any manner whatsoever without the express written permission of the respective writer of the respective poem/story except for the use of brief quotations in a book review. The writers of the respective works hold sole responsibility of the originality of the poems/stories and The Write Order is not responsible in anyway whatsoever.

Printed in India

ISBN: 978-93-90791-17-0

First Printing, 2021

The Write Order
Koramangala, Bangalore

Karnataka- 560029

THE WRITE ORDER PUBLICATIONS.

www.thewriteorder.com

Disclaimer

This is a work of fiction and doesn't intent to hurt religious or political sentiments of any person, community or group. Unless otherwise indicated, all the names, characters, businesses, places, events and incidents in this book are either the product of the author's imagination or used in a fictitious manner. Any resemblance to actual persons, living or dead, or actual events is purely coincidental.

Karpuura-Gauram

Karunna-Avataaram

Sansaara-Saaram

Bhujage[a-I]ndra-Haaram

Sadaa-Vasantam Hrdaya-Aravinde

Bhavam Bhavaanii-Sahitam Namaami|

Pure White like Camphor,
An Incarnation of Compassion,
The Essence of Worldly Existence,
Whose Garland is the King of Serpents,
Always Dwelling inside the Lotus of the Heart.
I Bow to Shiva and Shakti Together!!

'Shiva and Shakti are indistinguishable. They are one. They are the Universe. Shiva isn't masculine. Shakti isn't feminine. At the core of their mutual penetration the supreme consciousness opens.'

– Daniel Odier

Shiva beckons the call of Light,

It's ready to take flight,

Shiva ! Shiva! Shiva!

The name resounding as if nothing else astounds

Dancing and raising the head therein,

To know thyself and feelings therein,

Touching aspects of self to love wherein,

Shiva as the name astounds,

Shakti ascends to awaken all around.

The spiral journey begins to merge at the core

Shiva! Shiva! Shiva! Evolve

Shakti! Shakti! Shakti! Dissolve!

The molecules banging, the cells vibrating, the eternal dance

therein!

As the dance begins

Shakti rises to embrace Shiva

Shiva descends to embrace Shakti

SHIVA! SHIVA! SHIVA! SHIVA!

SHAKTI! SHAKTI! SHAKTI! SHAKTI!

The universal catastrophe begins

Each residing in the other

Each mating with the other

Each knowing other

Each palpitating with the other

Each dissolving with the other

Each mesmerized by the other

SHIVA, SHIVA, SHIVA, SHIVA

resides within!!!

SHAKTI, SHAKTI, SHAKTI, SHAKTI

rises within!!!!

I DEDICATE THIS BOOK TO MY SADGURU SAI BABA.

OM SAI RAM.

Contents

Preface	1
Chapter 1	3
Chapter 2	7
Chapter 3	11
Chapter 4	15
Chapter 5	19
Chapter 6	23
Chapter 7	27
Chapter 8	31
Chapter 9	35
Chapter 10	39
Chapter 11	43
Chapter 12	47
Chapter 13	51
Chapter 14	55
Chapter 15	59
Chapter 16	63

Chapter 17	67
Chapter 18	71
Chapter 19	75
Chapter 20	79
Chapter 21	83
Chapter 22	87
Chapter 23	91
Chapter 24	95
Chapter 25	99
Chapter 26	103
Chapter 27	107
Chapter 28	111
Chapter 29	115
Chapter 30	121
Chapter 31	125
Chapter 32	129
Chapter 33	133
Chapter 34	137
Chapter 35	143

CHAPTER 36	147
CHAPTER 37	151
CHAPTER 38	155
CHAPTER 39	159
CHAPTER 40	163
CHAPTER 41	167
CHAPTER 42	171
CHAPTER 43	175
CHAPTER 44	179
CHAPTER 45	185
CHAPTER 46	189
CHAPTER 47	193
CHAPTER 48	197
CHAPTER 49	201
CHAPTER 50	205
CHAPTER 51	209
CHAPTER 52	215
CHAPTER 53	221

I

Preface

This book came unexpectedly to me while I was working on two others, which still await completion. It suddenly began to dance in front of my eyes. I began to see images of Lord Shiva and Goddess Shakti and words to match the images just poured into my head. Beginning as one article that I posted on my WhatsApp groups and Facebook page, the overwhelming appreciation I received encouraged me to turn it into a book. And all the while, the words just kept pouring into my head, unbidden, unsought, and unconscious. Somehow I managed to scribble it all down as fast as it arrived. It's a completely channelled work and thus completely original with no reference to any other text or religious book. Shivhakti - The Continuous Continuum is not a religious discourse.

It is a spiritual and cosmic understanding of all that exists within and without. It is in everything around, we live and breathe it as explained in the text. The conversations between Lord Shiva and Goddess Shakti are illuminating and make the concept of Shiva Shakti--the divine masculine and the divine feminine so easy to understand. Hope you enjoy the book as much as I enjoyed writing it.

I am in deep gratitude to my Master Sai Baba and my Mother and Father God - Shiva and Shakti for making me a channel of their messages.

OM SAI RAM

Chapter 1

Shiva told Shakti, "I will test your love, I will behave indifferently, start haunting you and be unavailable. I will see how consistent you can be and how long you can wait in love. I will test your patience and see if your love is strong enough. To avoid judging me at my worst. I will disguise myself as a negative character and see if you can still recognize me."

Shakti replied "My love for you is ever true. I can see through all your disguises. My love can be and has been patient through eons of time. I have no fear of losing you because I know you are mine. I understand that the trick is not to get attached to your personality. I also understand I must not expect you to express your love, the way I like it; to understand your love whatever its expression is my test."

4

Shiva smiled and said "I am yours Shakti, come what may. I travel through time and space 'always to merge with your love. Together we can create. Together we can be powerful healers of light. I am your that half that you cannot live without. And you are my other half that I cannot exist without."

Shakti said "How much do you hide your feelings? Why don't you express your love for me? I have had to master the art of reading your thoughts to bear this period of separation and lack of demonstration. Why do you do that to me? Do you enjoy seeing me in pain?"

Shiva answers, "No my Beloved! It is my nature as a masculine. Demonstration of my feelings is not my strength. So I am flawed. But being with you I am learning to express and will master this art too. I will express and emote and you shall have no further complaints. I will make full efforts to add this to my divine masculine."

Shakti felt heard and respected. She was elated that Shiva had the patience to listen and understand her. She was feeling a sense of belonging back to him which was reflecting on her face that shone like a thousand stars shining in the dark sky. Shiva felt he was wrong in testing her love. The focus of any relationship should not be testing the other but on how to improve self and better the relationship. After all love can never be tested as love is plain and simple, always eternal and infinite.

They both felt a calmness descend on them and felt the bliss of union just in being together and looking into each other's eyes! Just in a moment of their unity of thoughts the love was so exhilarating that they both dived deep into the love consciousness becoming one with love.

6

Chapter 2

Shakti goes to the woods to meditate and Shiva goes searching for her. She is not available. Shiva wonders where she has gone. He finds her meditating in the woods. She looks gorgeous and is in a state of total ascension. He watches the beauty of her soul and he knows he is nothing without Shakti. He knows that Shakti is the source of the energy that flows through his body. He realizes that without Shakti he is [1]*Shava*. He waits till she arose from her dhyana. She was surprised to see asks, "[2]*Prannath*, what are you doing here? I would have come home soon."

Shiva says, "You are my strength and the life force flowing through me. Without you, I am nothing. I honor you and respect you always. I am not your 'prano ka nath'; in fact, you are my life and my happiness." Shakti smiled and said, "When did you come to this realization?"

[1]*Shava - A dead body
[2]* Prannath- Beloved

8

Shiva told her, "As I watched you sitting in dhyana. In your dhyana you were not meditating on any life source. You were the life source for the Earth, people, plant kingdom, animal kingdom. I saw that your 2*kan-kan exists in everything and I understood the dynamics of how I breathe you in and out. You are the energy we all breathe. You exist so we exist and you are so we are. Yet you do it so silently and unconditionally. You do not even get acknowledgement at times. I claim to be your prannath and you accept it so gracefully."

Shakti laughed and said "It is my nature as a mother to give, to nurture everything I come across. People who respect me get my strength and valor in a way they cannot even imagine. But I cannot have ego as I am the divine feminine and I flow invisible in the world as prana. Some call it energy, some call it prana, some call it chi. but it's only me Shakti. And you are my prannath. I am yours and I exist as you exist. We are one."

2*Kan-Kan - Your essence

Shiva smiles and asks, "I understand your role now and it is far greater than mine. I run this universe and you make it breathe."

Shiva bows down to Shakti and Shakti laughs and runs back home. Shiva runs after her knowing the strength she exuded in her daint demeanor. The external façade can be very distracting. He saw how power and strength could also be so gentle at the same time.

10

SHIVSHAKTI

Chapter 3

Sati's *(Shakti)* eyes are fixed on Shiva. She cannot understand the force that pulls her to him. She is so mesmerized by him. She cannot see his attire, his ways of living, the yogic life he leads. These aspects of him don't register with her at all. She cannot see beyond his essence of Shiva. She recognizes the connection of the souls, the bond and knows it to be far greater than anything she has ever known. Her senses give up on her and her heart skips a beat every time she sees Shiva.

Shiva, oblivious of her presence, is busy in his own activities, meditating and taking care of the universe. He is not interested in any of the games of love and is totally absorbed in spiritual [1]*sadhana*. He has no memory of Sati as his Beloved. He is in a trance, vibrating at the highest energies possible to provide the universe all it is required to play the game of illusions and karma.

[1]*Sadhana - Meditation

Sati meditates on her original form, the lingam- the symbol of their union and performs penance. She goes through her path of spiritual ascension to reach him and reminds him of his true love for her and thus begins the dance of the lovers. She reminds him that Love is the highest vibration possible and without Love the universe cannot exist. She shows him the realm of unconditional love which is like a pink sea of energy. They swim in that sea and awaken their senses to the love as pure as their very own essence that exists through eons of time. ShivShakti begin to dance in their eternal love union and the push and pull they create is for all lovers to remember the true essence of their Beloveds.

When they dance they transmute the energies of separation and pain into love and unity. The harmony created by them flows through the entire universe as Love. The push and pull creates illusions of pain and separation. And at the same time it ascends to unity through the hearts and souls of the lovers.

This lesson of love through the bridge of pain is greater than any lesson that can be learnt.

This push and pull may seem so unnecessary but it's the churning of the samundra manthan that will separate the ²*vish from ³*amruta and only then will only love remain as a prominent emotion and be recognized as true love.

In stillness, when centered if you can stay calm and focus only and only on Shiva and Shakti, you will notice the pain disappears as it is only an illusion for lovers to ascend to a higher vibration called Unconditional True Love.

²* Vish - Poison
³* Amruta - Ambrosia

14

Shivshakti

Chapter 4

Shiva lost his divinity and roamed the universe like a recluse. He indulged in different addictions and was immersed in his lower masculine ego. He did not realize that this drastic change in his personality was affecting the entire universe. He was lost in sensual pleasures and womanizing.

Seeing him thus Shakti felt a pang in her heart and was disheartened wondering how she could help him. She tried to restore his memories of his divinity which he had in some way forgotten. But she was unsuccessful in doing so. She was wondering how to bring him back.

Shiva was lost and needed to be brought back to a realization of his power. Since he had no understanding of what he was doing, it was only Shakti's presence of mind that could bring him back.

16

She was upset at why he was behaving in that manner. The lover in her was feeling hurt and betrayed and a part of her didn't want him back. She cried and cried. Just then, Lord Vishnu and Goddess Laxmi came to meet her. They asked her, "What's happened to you? You are a woman of such strength, the epitome of courage. Why have you suddenly become so weak?"

Shakti told them, "I am so in love with Shiva but after seeing him like this, I am hurt and upset with him and our relationship. Why has he gotten into these things? He is not Shiva anymore. But the strange thing is that despite being upset and perplexed with his behavior, my love for him has not lessened or weakened. Why is that so? I am trying so hard to walk away and leave him but it's just not possible. My love for him only grows."

Goddess Laxmi walks ahead towards Shakti, gesturing to Vishnu to let her answer this. She says, "Jagat Mata, Maa Shakti you are who you are and Shiva is who he is. He may be lost now but you also know it's only temporary. Even in this form, does he stop being Shiva? No!!! So how can he stop loving you and how can you stop loving him! The souls are one and will always remain one till eternity come what may. These separations are phases and will go away soon. They come as lessons and lead to growth. Love is all there is!"

Shakti smiles at them and they all move on to discussing how to remind Shiva of his divinity and bring him back into his authentic self.

SHIVSHAKTI

Chapter 5

The early Morning sunrise is always a sight to behold. The sun's rays falling on the Mansarovar Mountain look like they are bowing down to the mountain and enveloping it in chants of "Shiva, Shiva, Shiva!!"

The entire mountain echoes to the sound of the name of Lord Shiva and Shakti lying half - awake on her bed, seeing the mountain from her window, she smiles and feels blessed being there with her beloved. But it had not been an easy ride. She underwent many years of [1]*tapasya* and worked on her own inner divinity to merge with Shiva as Parvati. It has been a very long journey.

Shiva too feels gratitude when he sees Shakti in his abode and wonders how he had even survived so long without her. No wonder he became a yogi as no one else had enticed him so much.

[1]*Tapasya - Penance

Nothing interested him as much as she did. He had eyes only for her. She kept him happy and elated. He was more than happy to listen to the sound advice she gave him about his work of running the world. He always felt so balanced and elevated with her. She was truly his Beloved.

But there was a time when they both didn't recognize their mutual love. When Shakti had seen Shiva she felt a strange pang in her heart. The knowingness had felt like home to her every time she saw him. She just knew she was born to marry him. Yet the family she was born in and her [2]*sakhis* didn't allow her to remember her journey. She kept asking herself what it was that was pulling her towards him. His simple persona was very unusual, in fact strange, his attire made him very different from the normal person. He had a different enigma to him. There was a certain magnetic pull in him that kept her mesmerized. He did not fit in anywhere in the framework of the groom her parents were seeking for her. The conflict within confused her and she could not understand why it

[2]*Sakhis - Friend

was that she kept thinking only of Shiva. She didn't understand why she felt so attracted to him. It was like a voice from the soul saying, "Shakti, he is the one. He is the other half of your soul."

She wouldn't understand what these voices in her head were saying. She would lie awake all night looking at the moon and wondering where her destiny would take her. And Shiva on the other hand was a yogi, least interested in a family. He loved his Light and loved to meditate in his light. He did not like being disturbed in his meditation.

Both had to break their inner conditioning, stubborn patterns, social comfort zones and fears. They had to break certain beliefs and gather the courage to stand up for their truth. Shakti had to face up to her family, her kingdom; she had to disappoint her parents and the people of the kingdom to come together in full union as two halves to make a whole. It was a difficult task that required great courage. Many don't make it so far. But Shakti was determined to fulfill the task she had taken upon herself at birth and she completed it to her full capacity. Shiva had no choice but to shed his beliefs and embrace his true love.

Coming back to the present, they both embraced each other, happy that they had made certain choices even if it went against tradition and comfort zones and broke the hearts of many close family members. The family eventually accepted them seeing their love. They breathed a sigh of relief and looked at the snow-clad mountains and the blue sky beyond to the unlimited vastness.

Yes! Life is full of unlimited possibilities! One just has to have the courage to reach out to them.

Chapter 6

Shakti asked Shiva, "Why do you always sit in meditation. What are you showing your devotees? That they should also leave their households and come to the mountains to meditate. How is that possible? Shouldn't you set a better example for them? You always look so calm with your eyes shut and body still. What is the secret, please tell me. How do others achieve it?"

Shiva smiled and told Shakti, "It seems very calm and serene. But have you experienced the climate of the mountains. It is cold and harsh and ever-changing, the most severe conditions to exist amidst. By sitting here in my bare attire and in this calm state, the message that I send to all is that come what may, however harsh your lot, always maintain your calmness and inner centre. Only then can you retain the courage and power to face all situations and handle them. The cold snowy mountains are akin to the cold selfish people around you. Be so centered and aligned with your higher self that these things and people don't matter to you. Do not allow your state of mind to go up and down with the circumstances. Never allow yourself to become too happy or too sad. Once you learn to brave the coldness and anger around you and stay grounded in your emotions, nothing can touch you. You can then be bare chested even in the snow like me, which means your true authentic self without the masks and yet smiling in a deep meditative state. My dear Shakti, this is how I pass my message to the people."

Shakti was very happy to hear the answer and she went around doing her work. Suddenly there was an earthquake and the mountains started shaking. Shakti immediately arose, sensing som danger or an attack and took her original form as Maa Durga with all her weapons handy but within a few minutes the violent shaking stopped and she wondered what had happened.

Shiva rose from his asana and walked towards her smiling. He told her, "And you are an example of how in spite of staying calm and centered, whenever there is a sense of danger your whole strength and courage should concentrate on fiercely laying down their boundaries and not allowing anyone to walk over you, come what may. Good people are always walked over and taken for granted. Givers are always asked to give more. Shakti, your persona is a perfect example of how gentle and nurturing you can one be one minute and how strong and courageous another. You always maintain the balance between your inner calmness and inner strength."

Shakti smiled and said, "Yes Prannath! Together we show the world a perfect example of how one's inner Shivshakti should emerge. We reside in each and every one - our form of love, mature thought, strength, creativity and resilience. One just needs to look within and accept all the qualities of one's truest self and one's shivshakti will emerge. Each of the people around us is part of us. I bow to you and me. I bow to us. I bow to our oneness."

And they both held hands and walked towards their home to find warmth within each other, as they were each other's strength and love, expanding consciousness forever and ever.

Chapter 7

Shiva and Sati *(Shakti)* loved to be together. When they were together, life seemed magical as if time had stopped and there was no one and nothing around them. Just the two of them. The magnetic pull between them seemed tremendous, like a huge power house which created great energy that could heal the universe and the Earth. Life seemed bliss. Who knew that it would be short-lived. When your own parents do not understand your life path and your soul's essence, it is very difficult to get there. The blessings of parents are as important as air to breathe.

King Daksha *(Sati's Father)* was so full of ego that he did not recognize the divinity and aura of Shiva. He couldn't look beyond outer appearance and challenged Sati's choice even after he got them married on her insistence. He was not happy with Shiva as a son-in-law. For him, tradition, worldly wisdom, a materialistic life and riches were more important. He judged Shiva through this prism and thought he was a failure in life. He couldn't see Shiva's amazing inner light. He saw Shiva with his eyes and couldn't connect with his inner self.

When King Daksha held a grand yagna, he did not invite Shiva as he felt embarrassed to introduce Shiva as his son-in-law. This hurt Sati badly as she was in so much in love with Shiva. She required her father's approval and for him to love Shiva as he loved her. She felt incomplete without her father's acknowledgement and felt it was her duty to show him the divinity Shiva held within. She chose to go to the yagna without Shiva only with the intention of convincing her father. But King Daksha in his grand ego did not like Sati *(Shakti)* waxing eloquent about her husband and they ended up arguing fiercely. In her anger, she jumped into the yagna, (in that moment her anger was so great, she didn't think of the consequences). She didn't think about how Shiva would live without her.

When the news reached Shiva that Sati *(Shakti)* had immolated herself in the sacrificial fire, he felt both deep anger/rage and the pain of separation, along with multiple other emotions of a wide spectrum. Sati *(Shakti)* had awakened that love in him that he never knew existed. And now she was gone. The pain that Shiva felt was unbearable. They had not yet learnt the art of detached love and had yet another lifetime ahead to learn it. He was so angry that he destroyed the whole yagna shala and beheaded King Daksha. He was so enraged that he took the [1]*shava* of Sati *(Shakti)* and roamed the earth and skies doing the tandava which would have caused an apocalypse but Lord Vishnu intervened to stop Shiva from destroying the world.

This made Sati's *(Shakti)* body disintegrate into 52 parts and fall all over the earth. It's a symbol of great love that never dies.

Lives after life, lovers learn the lessons of love and expand creation. Truly it is only love that exists!!!

[1]*Shava - Dead Body

SHIVSHAKTI

Chapter 8

ShivShakti, a name, an energy, a cycle, creation, a magnanimous universe of its own. The name itself says it all. Two halves make one whole. Two equals make one circle of light. Neither one less neither one more. Each one has its own attributes and own strengths and own weaknesses complementing each other. Each one is making the other strong and weak at the same time. It's like a game. A push and a pull which ends up becoming a dance of ShivShakti. They dance together in complete harmony, creating energy for growth and learning, expansion and enlightenment.

The separation that exists between them is nothing but an illusion created by the darkness. Once you shed light on it, you will notice that there is no separation. Each one is seeking the other and yet each one is complete in its own aspect. The tiny thread that connects the two is the life force that keeps them going, which keeps pumping in as much energy as needed to keep the dance of life going.

What is needed is to stop the pull and push and maintain stillness. In stillness, that which you seek shall come to you as both are aspects of one flame and have to be attracted to its magnet. The inner stillness of Shakti will always bring Shiva to her always without fail and Shiva has no choice but to respond to Shakti's call. It's like self calling self. It's like two halves of the self becoming whole again and then dividing again and uniting yet again for life to go on.

The force of Shivshakti has to complete 108 cycles to come to stillness and then again, after maintaining stillness, it goes to the next level like a game. It keeps raising its level and plays again, each time going deeper and deeper into its own consciousness to gain more expansion and reach different dimensions of life. Each dimension has its set of rules, beliefs and conditioning which need to be dealt with.

As Shivshakti ascends, it leads the universe to a better and larger truth of self. The Shiva energy expands and rises up to encompass all it comes across in its way. Together they are a life force, the Ida Pingala nadi which when united is the Sushumna nadi. The microcosm reflects the macrocosm and vice versa. Shivshakti is the atom and molecules within us. The Anu and Renu which keep dividing further but still maintains its oneness always. Shivshakti reigns the universe and every beat of the heart of mother earth.

Shivshakti is present in the sky and earth; as above so below. It's in everything you can see around. It exists in you. It exists in me. It exists in us!!!

My Shiva merged with me today!

I am in a complete trance,

With no words to say,

Shiva and Shakti are one today!!!!

ANITA RAJANI

Chapter 9

Shiva was not born of anyone; he is Swayambhu while Maa Shakti had to manifest herself as the daughter of a king. She has many forms. You see her but she is an energy that cannot be contained. Then why did she choose to be born in a kingdom and merge with Shiva eventually. She is the omnipresent Maa Shakti and yet she chose to take a human form and then rise to her own divinity. She shows us how to ascend from being human to an ever-expanding energy. This is what ascension is all about.

Shakti made many choices in her life as a king's daughter. She chose to be King Daksha's daughter as Sati *(Shakti)*, so one day Shiva could behead the ego of her King Daksha and bring sanity to the Earth. He was later resurrected with the head of a goat after he asked for forgiveness from Shiva. She chose to be King Himavat's daughter so that she could practice discipline and hardships to attain her Shiva. Parvati's life journey to merge with

Shiva was not an easy one. She had to take birth as a daughter to her parents and then break the boundaries of conditioning and traditional social systems, helping to break them in the collective consciousness of humanity. Shakti was always fully focused on Shiva and her knowingness kept her intentions very high and powerful and her faith very strong.

Only through ascetic discipline could she attain her goals which could help her merge with Shiva. So why did Shakti, the epitome of strength and valor as Durga or her many other different forms need to work her way up to Shiva. It was a leela they performed for us to understand the importance of patience, resilience, discipline and faith in one's goals to reach the Beloved. So many give up on the way or choose the easier way, worried about the wrath of other humans. So many lack the courage to choose the truth of their own souls.

The feminine principle is being taught to be resilient and strong and attain Shiva through the tough ascetic discipline which she portrayed. The divine feminine principle when she goes through the process only emerges stronger and more compassionate in her heart to represent the mother principle. Shivshakti the father-mother God of the universe in their leela have portrayed a life through which we learn and understand how to move forward in tough times when illusions seem larger than truths, when faith falters and patience is tested.

The stories of Shivashakti bring the understanding that truth always wins. Once the truth is achieved then peace prevails. If there is no peace, it means the journey has not ended and there is more to achieve. Keep walking till one attains peace. The end of the road is always peace and harmony.

The peace within should be the criterion to understand if you have attained your inner Shivshakti balance.

Have you??

ANITA RAJANI

SHIVSHAKTI

Chapter 10

I have been constructed by someone out of half your body; Therefore there is no difference between us, and my heart is in you. Just as my Self, heart, and life has been placed in you, So has your Self, heart, and life been placed in me.

- Brahma

Being together complementing each other makes them whole. Two halves that are complete in togetherness with each other. Shivshakti - Father God and Mother God - have created this universe with their unity and essence of one - the Ardhanareshwara Roopa. The whole universe breathes this essence. For every form of Shiva there is an equivalent form of Shakti. She is equal with him in all aspects of her personality. Shakti and Shiva complements each other in every way. But every aspect or form of Shakti has always faced the brunt and the Shiva aspect has also equally borne the pain even if that side of the story is not known to mankind.

Sati *(Shakti)* underwent a lot of ¹*tapasya* and the wrath of her own father to marry Shiva and so her tests seems far greater, but the Shiva energy as her counterpart has always been holding her space so she could achieve this. Parvati also had to evolve in her consciousness and attain her goals. It would not have been possible without Shiva's trust and the faith he built in her for him.

Reality shows the Shakti principle is doing most of the work to attain unity. But that's not so, it's always both ways never one. As one evolves the other too is evolving. Radha and Krishna are another aspect of Shivshakti. If Radha bore the pain of separation, so did Krishna. He seemed to be married and happy but not a day passed without him thinking of Radha. She was in every cell of his body. And so was Meera, as Meera was just another form of the same Radha experiencing separation and learning the art of devotion. Sita too had to support Rama in everything he did. She

---

¹*Tapasya - Penance

sacrificed her life of riches to be with Rama rather than bear the pain of separation from him. Rama also sacrificed his riches. If later he banished her from the kingdom, there was not a day he spent in happiness. He was bearing the pain of separation just like Sita was learning the art of unconditional love.

This separation teaches them that the physical presence is not important and that the other half of you will always exist in you, come what may. What Shakti will experience through separation Shiva too has to experience. There is no escape. So neither sacrificed more or less; both felt the same pain and the same love and that's the true meaning of Shivshakti. It may seem that Shiva just sat on his asana and Shakti made her way up to the goal. However, Shiva had to be still to allow Shakti to come to him. Sitting still is as difficult as waiting, as difficult as climbing up to her lover for merger. If he wouldn't have sat still, she wouldn't have managed the climb. It's like two sides of the same coin. It's just the role each one plays to merge with the other. That's the true form of Shivshakti.

It creates a trust so implicit in each other that the logic will not be able to hold back the love and union is the only way to end this game. Everything else seems meaningless.

It is Shivshakti that is the ultimate truth of mankind!!

Chapter 11

ShivShakti also has another form - the sacred lingam. Shiva and Shakti are so one in that form that you cannot make out one from the other. It is a task to discern them separately and their union is so sacred that one can only bow down to its divinity. It is a form of unity and oneness which can be understood by placing one's head to take darshana. Its energy when absorbed by humans changes the karmic imbalance of yin and yang within you. It is Shivshakti intertwined with each other like two snakes coiled into each other. When the Shivshakti stays combined in energy like the lingam, it is the perfect energy created for manifestation and healing the world. That's why there are so many lingams across the country.

The twelve Jyotirlingas all over the country are placed on the grid of the earth in such a way as to spread healing and positive energy across the land to maintain its sacredness. There are thousands of lingam temples for the same reason. They receive the energy of

Shivshakti and transfer it into the land and energize it to create a continuously evolving space. The significance of the lingams is very clear and they are the most sacred space of the earth. Jyotirlinga means radiant light. The radiance of the lingam is so bright that it can heal the soul's karmic imbalance and create a healing space within. The main Jyotirlingas are twelve in number as the number twelve is important in the sacred space—twelve months in a year, twelve followers of Jesus, etc. The number is considered holy and sacred in many religions.

Shakti asks Shiva, "Why are we represented in the form of a lingam?" Shiva replies, "This is the best way to show oneness as sacred union as it is the direct road to moksha, to ascension. How else to depict this union to humans? They still live in darkness and look upon union as fun and lust. What they don't realize is that by sacred union with your partner you can achieve enlightenment and pure bliss." Shakti asked, "How will you ensure that they reach their enlightenment or understand what this lingam means and how to meditate on it?"

Shiva walked towards Shakti and looked into her eyes with so much love that she felt overwhelmed with the love of her Shiva that filled the heart, completing her and enhancing her essence as Maa Shakti. He told her, "My Beloved, that's not my job. As the soul will ascend, they will see the divine truth as the truth never hides itself, it just needs the eye to see it. Once the illusions that lock a soul in worldly desires begin to drop, as people chant my or your name they will see the truth as it is, nothing more and nothing less. That's when they will integrate it within themselves and use it for their ascension and that's when no soul on Earth will again misuse or disrespect such sacred unions. Then there will be no betrayals, no rapes. Also there will be only divine marriages."

He added, "Once they feel the essence of the lingam there will be no false marriages or relationships based on material benefits. There will be a place of bliss where Shivshakti will reside in each one and they will respect and love each other and unite for eternity."

Satisfied with Shiva's reply, Shakti was assured of his intention towards the Earth and its inhabitants. She shut her eyes and sat down for her dhyana.

Chapter 12

When two energies reach the point of complete merger where they can no longer exist beyond and without each other, they are not codependent souls having major problems with each other and undergoing unity and separation. They are interdependent souls co- existing - independent yet in a merger. They are aware of their boundaries and yet are boundary-less. They don't face any problems without each other and yet are always with each other in everything they do and in every breath. Yet the physical separation doesn't cause pain or agony. They reach a point where the knowingness is complete and none of the lower self issues exists.

Both had resolved every karmic aspect of self and each is a light body at the same level of awareness, mirroring each other through their actions and emotions. Emotions don't escalate or dip. Logic doesn't overpower or remain dormant. Both emotions and logic coexist in the same realm, respecting each other's boundaries. Just as Shiva holds the moon in his *jata*, a metaphor for balanced emotions.

Shakti holds the lotus in her hands representing her ascension despite all hardships. Both represent the emotional and spiritual aspects of love.

Love thrives in all aspects and doesn't grow lesser at any stage of evolution. The lotus represents the essence of love in all circumstances good or bad and by holding the lotus Shakti shows that however difficult the environment, her love for Shiva thrives and grows every single day. She acknowledges her masculine aspect and yet retains her gentleness.

The moon in his [1]*jata* represents that the masculine Shiva acknowledges his emotions, his feminine aspect, to its fullest and has a hold over himself and is grounded and stable always.

---

[1]*Jata - Lock of hair

Both have shown respect and love for each other. When they look into each other's eyes they know the souls are one and the maturity of the emotions allows them to live a life unconditionally with each other compromising and sacrificing in their own glory with a smile and understanding of each other's divinity. The souls shine as one and as the other half all at once.

Both are one and the same after all. Are they not?

Ardhanarishwara - another form of the union of Shivshakti.

I exist within you and you exist within me.
I breathe you and you breathe me.
We are in unity all along and in total awareness of consciousness!!

Chapter 13

Shiva and Shakti held hands and were walking along the banks of Mansarovar lake. They seem so content, happy and divinely aligned with each other. Their unconditional support for each other had made each feel complete and [1]*paripoorna* from within. Shiva smiled and asked Shakti, "What is it that a man needs to be happy?"

With a mischievous gleam in her eyes, Shakti said, "A woman". They both knew he meant a soul and they both laughed at her humour. Then she replied seriously, "A man needs constant connection with his God/ Divine Light, a disciplined habit or prayers/ connect with his Lord so he is guided at all times. Else he is like a man on the road without a road map, lost, not knowing which direction to take. But once he is in touch with his God/ Higher self he will get constant guidance on what to do next, what

[1]*Paripoorna - Complete

to choose and on the results of the choices he makes. Else he will end up taking the wrong road, diversions and in chaos."

Shiva replied, "True, my beloved. Your answer is very apt. Now tell me what keeps a man in suffering?" Shakti replied, "His desires, his ego, his inability to surrender to God, his mind and the karmic darkness around him keep him in constant suffering. If he can live a life of discipline, controlling his needs, wants and desires and leading a simple life of few materialistic desires, free of lust, greed and hate and be humble, he will be happier and attain moksha easily."

She further added, "Shiva, look at you, such a simple life, without desires and focused simply on upliftment of your devotees and the earth. Look at your needs: you wear a simple loin cloth, rudrakshas and 2*bhasm on your body. How minimalistic your life is. And see me, I am happy living in the mountain caves with bare necessities. Each human needs to evolve to this level.

2*Bhasm - Ashes

That's what we represent - Shivshakti abundant in our simplicity and our eternal love for each other. It's enough to stay happy."

Shiva was enjoying the discussion with her. These brainstorming sessions gave them both much clearer perspectives about many things. They discussed in complete equality sans their genders, ego, and personalities coming in the way. They believed in the concept of allowance of different perspectives and making space to push views out of the box so new boundaries can be created.

They kept walking along the healing and divine Lake Mansarovar, energizing it with their powers to help the world. They enjoyed these small adventures together. It kept the spark going.

SHIVSHAKTI

Chapter 14

Shiva carrying his *Trishul* and Nandi by his side goes towards Shakti who also has a trishul in her hand and her lion walking beside her. They always look at each other with so much love that they can melt instantly into each other. The love that emanates from their hearts for each other is like sparks of fire raising the passion and desire to merge with each other. The magnetism is so powerful that they can instantly merge into a union. But they hold themselves as they have tasks to accomplish.

Just at that moment Narad Muni- the messenger of God comes to visit them. They acknowledge his presence and ask him why has he come, and what the purpose of his visit is. Narayan says, "Hey Shiv Shamboo and Jagat Mata, I had a thought that disturbed me and was wondering if you could give me some clarity on it."

Shakti replies, "Hey Narad Muni, we would be only too happy. Please tell us what is on your mind?" Then Narad Muni asks, "Why do you, Shiva the masculine, ride a Nandi while Maa rides a Lion? Please do not be offended by my question but I have been wondering about it and couldn't think of an answer."

Shiva felt a little annoyed but calmed himself down first and then replied, "Narad Muni, it's your male ego that makes you ask such an absurd question. Never again indulge your ego as you belong to the realm of Devas and you need to be evolved and not think of such petty things. Nevertheless, I will reply to your question. My Nandi, which I ride is a bull and a bull is a symbol of righteousness and masculine energy. It's very important that your actions should be righteous. Whereas, the lion which my beloved rides signifies strength and power. The true power lies with Shakti, the feminine aspect. It's a reminder for all to be righteous and not have any male ego and the divine consciousness will always support you. The other reminds you to always retain your strength and power come what may and use it only when required and stay humble. So my dear friend, that's the reason we have these two ¹*vahanas* to ride respectively."

Narad Muni smiles and bows down to Shiva saying, "Narayan, Narayan, I expected a very humble and intelligent answer and I got one. Oh! Shiva and Mata, I hope all humanity arises to your level of consciousness one day and merges back into you. Isn't that the ultimate goal of each human? Isn't that what moksha is all about?"

To this, Shakti said, "Brother Narad Muni, I would like to remind you that Masculine ego or a feminine vanity doesn't exist in the Shivshakti consciousness and that is why we chose our respective vahanas with much thought. It's not a false mask to show someone or misguide them. As role models we always have to represent the truth and existence depends on our truth which becomes the universal truth. There is no place for negative qualities in our personalities. We are Shivshakti and we have reached here by

¹*Vahanas - Vehicle

understanding the true dynamics of this energy. It doesn't behove you to judge us either. We come from a consciousness which permeates all humanity and every cell of the universe. Each and every planet revolving around the earth and the sun, the moon, all stars thrive on the energy of the Shivshakti."

Narayan bowed his head and asked for their forgiveness and left. He left satisfied that he had the perfect answer to give if someone asked such petty questions. He wanted to know so he could silence them. He walked away to his space with a smile and heart full of love for Shivshakti as even being in their presence gave one a heart full of a lifetime of love.

The level of infinite consciousness that existed within Shivshakti was enough for the entire world for eons to come. It was enough to evoke righteousness, truth, strength and valour in all but always combined with unconditional love. What a wonderful amalgam!!!

Chapter 15

When Shiva flows in Shakti and Shakti flows in Shiva, they make a complete circle just like the yin and yang symbol. Half black and half white with the opposite color circle in between. That's what a complete circle, a complete soul, a complete shunya is. Nothingness traveling into everything and everything traveling back into nothingness, moving back and forth in complete rhythm and that is called Life/ Breath.

Shakti resides below the heart, Shiva resides above the heart and the heart is where they blend as equals, as the yin and yang, as Shivshakti in all its aspects and glory. Shakti is the Mother God and Mother earth represented in the kundalini energy and Shiva is the Father God and Sky God representing the energy in the crown chakra. When Kundalini maa rises up, the shushmna nadi uniting the Ida and Pingala, right and the left, Shiva and Shakti rise as one energy from the base/ root of a man towards the crown clearing karmic residue in each aspect/ chakra/ organ of the body. Once it reaches the crown and the crown opens up all its thousand petals to form a higher dimensional realm, one can become a co-creator with God.

Shivshakti created this universe and it is Shivshakti that can destroy it. It takes many forms to do the needful and help the world. Shiva asked Shakti, "I reside in you and you reside in me. We are always in each other. So why do you feel the separation at times when I am lost in my own world, in my 1*dhyana*. Why do you slide from feeling 2*paripoorna* to feeling an incomplete self? Aren't we always in each other? Does the circle of yin and yang ever become half? Even if it becomes half, the small circle will always remain with the other, so what happens?"

1*Dhyana - Meditation
2*Paripoorna - Completeness

Shakti told him. "Prannath, I am our feminine aspect. I am the one who is more patient and resilient and can take the backseat to play a supportive role. And that can be easily taken for granted. I can easily be walked over as I am the mother and the unconditional love within me makes the masculine at times think I am forever available. So when you are in dhyana or focusing on your inner self, you do not pay any thought to me, knowing that I shall stay forever by your side, come what may. I have done ³*tapas* at all levels to come here to be with you. I have left the existence of my birth and my family to be with you. You, on the other hand, haven't done any of this for me so naturally when you withdraw, my whole existence is shaken as my sense of belonging comes from you. I do not want to be taken for granted. You must also understand that even I can leave you. But that's not possible."

³*Tapas - Sacrifices*

62

The unconditional love that flows from me to you will never ever give you that insecurity. But your masculine love does not flow to me with the same degree of unconditional love, although it's a love full of support, care and protection. So I naturally feel shaken if you withdraw.

Shiva understands Shakti's feminine love and honors her immediately by affirming that he will always keep her with him even when he withdraws into his being so she doesn't feel the void.

Chapter 16

With this whole game of ¹*samsara* from primordial times, Shivshakti has been evolving at a continuous level. The consciousness of Shivshakti manifests itself in many different ways and forms. Every form has its own evolution and manifests itself as evolved matter which ultimately again merges into the primal matter and expansion takes place. It's this whole breaking of matter into parts and evolving and merging back again into the prime force that life and human life is all about.

Many times due to veils, original existence is forgotten and darkness takes over and works through matter, causing negative forces to evolve. But Shivshakti in the form of Rudrakali is manifested to destroy any such creation. There is a constant spurging taking place and constant evaluation of where the energy has reached. This causes the ²*Anu* and *Renu* of matter to do their ³*Tandava* and expand continuously. And that's how the life force

¹*Samsara - Cycle of birth and death
²*Anu and Renu - Atom and Molecule
³*Tandava - Divine dance

that keeps us alive gets continuously created. It is like a big heart pumping blood in and out into the entire living world, the heart being made up of two energies Shiva and Shakti- Anu and Renu. This heart is the microcosm of the macrocosm.

At the beginning of time, when the first life force was created to construct this entire universe and its game, it was Shivshakti together that created that first speck of life. Now too they are constantly creating life with their united breath. Even if one doesn't exist with or without the other. The illusions created around the whole concept are to keep it protected from forces that will not allow it to unite. It needs to be felt to be understood. It cannot be seen.

Can you see air? Can you see energy? Can you see the life force? You cannot as it is not for the eyes to see and it doesn't need to be visible. It is an intelligent space which is created to show what is necessary and to feel what is necessary.

When you can feel it and understand the unity, you have truly reached the stage of transformation and inner unity.

*Each one of you is a Shivshakti and each one of you can achieve the same inner unity that is shown to you but what you need is 4*tapasya and 5*sadhana. Only then can your heart open up and align with the Father and Mother God. And attain just bliss!!!*

4*Tapasya - Sacrifice
5*Sadhana - Meditation

Chapter 17

It is very important to chant the name of the Lord every single moment. Chant and meditate on Shiva and automatically you are meditating on Shakti. Meditate on Shakti and Shiva's grace will follow. It is a combined loop like the infinity symbol. The symbol carries the energies of Shiva and Shakti into each other. It flows in and out of each other in a never-ending infinite loop of the infinite world and cosmos.

Shiva cannot live without Shakti. He may not express or emote the way Shakti does as emotions are the forte of the divine feminine. He will only be silent as he feels showing your vulnerability is being weak. He may stay silent and suffer within and not allow it to show while Shakti wonders, "What has happened? Does he not feel as deeply as me? Why do I always seem to be expressing my love for him? My love is like worship and I am dedicated to him and him alone. For me, he is my life, my breath and my life force but he seems so silent, always meditating and at peace with himself. He thinks of worldly matters and how to run this ¹*shrishti.

Shiva heard her thoughts as if it got echoed to him through telepathy through the united energy fields of the infinite loop. He woke up from the meditative space and broke his ²*sadhna. He could feel what she felt while she could also feel what he felt. Shiva empathized with her restlessness and went up to her. She was surprised to see him and asked him, "Prannath, why have you broken your sadhna and come, what's the matter. Are you ok?" Shiva's blue eyes pierced into her dark hazel ones and held her in an embrace. He told her, "Shakti, I also feel as you as I am also the part of the infinite loop. The feelings of both are flowing to each other constantly and infinitely. That's what makes you and me a perfect symbol of infinity. Our bond is eternal. What has made you so restless? Your calmness and peace helps me meditate and look after shrishti. And your restlessness makes me restless too.

¹*Shristi - Universe
²*Sadhana - Meditation

Your every cell vibrates my name and so does my every cell vibrate your name. I do not express as my expression is in action but I also worship you and your existence my Devi. I am because you are."

Shakti smiled contentedly and said, "And Prannath I am because you are. Thank you for this wonderful gesture and for reminding me of our infinite and eternal love that permeates and exists in every beat and cell of this universe. Just a bit of silence and everyone can hear it as all existence is this love. The entire universe is created out of this love between you and me. And together we thrive. Our heartbeats are connected to every being that exists on the earth, every plant and the mineral kingdom too. Yes, now I can see once again all that exists is just you and me." And they held their embrace to seal their love forever once again.

ANITA RAJANI

Shiva added, "Humanity has forgotten it is a by - product of the love of Shivshakti and has begun to feel it is the power. It has begun the journey of destroying all that was made out of love. See it selfishly using the resources given to it to thrive as if they have created it and it won't end ever. It has begun to take it all for granted and thoroughly abuse it. Whenever humanity loses the consciousness of love and the source from which it has emerged, I Shiva, begin the game of destruction through various modes. Then it has no choice but to turn back to me and remember that it is but a strand of Shakti and me and cannot let ego blind it. The pain and suffering inflicted upon it is only to bring it back to my infinite loop of Shivshakti love. A reminder of where it belongs. It's real home!!!"

It was a moment of exhilarating truth energy vibrating across the cosmos. The real home is where Shivshakti resides!

Chapter 18

Shiva and Shakti were resting and suddenly they heard a loud thudding sound. They both woke up and went out to the courtyard to see what had happened and saw a huge creature lying half dead on the ground. They ran to him and asked him who he was. He replied, "Oh, [1]*Jagatpita*, I am a monster and have been bad all my life and now I am about to die. My life is about to end. I have come to ask you to rescue me. Once I die, I do not want to go to the realm of demons. I want to get [2]*moksha* and evolve into a higher level of soul. My soul was yearning for your [3]*darshana* and I am so happy now that I have seen you both Mother and Father God of this [4]*shrishti*. I am very happy and know I will get a place at your holy feet and a different birth next time. My demonic soul is asking for evolution. Would you kindly grant me the evolution of my soul?"

[1]*Jagatpita - Father God
[3]*Darshana - Visit

[2]*Moksha - Enlightenment
[4]*Shristi - Universe

72

Shakti held his head on her lap like a mother and stroked him with love. The monster looked at with tear-filled eyes and asked her, "Mother! How can you be so compassionate and non-judgmental? I have been a monster and have been doing what I am supposed to do. I have somehow made my way up to you both. I have realized that my actions have caused much harm and my lower energies have created major destruction in Mother Earth's energy fields. Yet you stand here stroking me in such a motherly manner. It makes me want to die faster in my guilt. But my love for you both and seeing you 5*_sakshaat_ is keeping me alive so I can earn your grace. Please tell me how do you both stay so much larger than life and with such an evolved consciousness. How can I gain ascension in my next birth and how can I speed up the process to be with you both. I am a sinner but the love flowing from you both to me is healing every broken and unclean aspect of me."

5*Sakshaat - In real

Shiva replied, "Where Shiva and Shakti reside, no evil can even enter. You have so much repentance that you have cleared much of your energies and karma and that evolution made it possible for you to reach us. The master appears when the student is ready. You are now ready to embark on the journey of light. And the first lesson of Light is Love which you learnt here right now before even ending this monster lifetime. You will embark on the journey of a bird and shower love upon all. Your energies will portray love."

The monster shut his eyes and passed away in bliss with the knowingness of the greatest kind of unconditional love - the love of a mother and father combined. How profound it felt!

How the love of mother and father can complete anyone and heal them fully! Even in the highest dimensions, the journey of unconditional love begins with parental love!

SHIVSHAKTI

Chapter 19

Shakti was walking around the hill and the tinkling sound of her [1]*payals* echoed in the valleys. Shiva even in his sadhana smiled as the sound made him happy. Her feminine grace overflowing into everything, Shakti looked stunning even in her simple attire. Shiva sat content as Shakti was moving around their abode in Kailasa gracefully, spreading her nurturing energy all around. Maa Laxmi and Maa Saraswati came to visit her and asked, "Shakti, your form is so graceful and yet you wear only flowers as adornment and live such a simple mountainous life. Don't you desire the jewels that you wore as a princess, as the daughter of a king. How have you managed to overcome your desires and make sure that they don't manage to sneak into your mind unbidden?"

Shakti smiled and said, "Oh my dear sisters, what are jewels?" They replied in unison, "Jewels are a woman's happiness and pride."

[1]*Payals - Trinklets

Shakti asked, "Are they more important than your Beloved's love?" They both looked at her wide-eyed, trying to digest what she was saying. Shakti continued with a wise demeanor, "Let me explain! Many feminine in their need for good homes, acceptance in their own families, comfort zones and need for luxuries, give up on true love. For them it's more important that their families accept their Beloved and their clothes, ornaments, etc. are in tune with what is socially desirable. They can't compromise on their lifestyle and so end up in marriages that give them everything but true love and thereby true happiness. They make a bargain for a lifetime because they don't have the courage to embrace their true self, their true feelings, and their soul's authenticity. They feel scared of the unknown. They don't trust their heart and don't follow their intuition. Basically, they have abandoned their feminine aspect and embraced the masculine logical aspect. When they learn to trust their inner voice, when the eyes of their beloved are adornment enough, when their Beloved's embrace is better than the richest dress and their Beloved's smile is their peace and they don't need any false masks, then they won't need any false homes, false friends and worldly riches to make them happy. They will find peace and happiness. And that's what I have found my true self and my true happiness. I do not need any ornaments, clothes or anything artificial and to be unauthentic to keep me happy. I am 2*paripoorna in my love for my beloved."

And the three of them embrace each other and Maa Saraswati and Maa Lakshmi feel Shakti's happiness flowing to them too. They are able to deeply understand her feelings.

Shakti had found Unity and Godhood within herself. She has integrated her wise self and she is the true Shakti of her Shiva. The simplicity mirrors wisdom and feeling of being complete within one's own soul without needing anything else to fulfill self. In true words, Love is enough!

2*Paripoorna - Complete

Chapter 20

Sati *(Shakti)* was undergoing penance. She was walking in the forest when she came across a sage. He looked at her simple attire sans the jewels that should adorn a princess. He was an old sage and knew instantly who she was and what process she was undergoing. As soon as Sati *(Shakti)* saw the sage she bowed down at his holy feet. He blessed her and asked her, "Dear child, why do you look so stressed and worried? Can I help in any way?"

Sati *(Shakti)* replied, "Yes Guruji! I am much stressed. When I see Shiva he is my Beloved. I can say for sure there can be no other for me except Shiva. A thousand lamps light up in my heart, my physical body emanates a beautiful perfume and I can't take my eyes off him when I see him. I lose all my words and go silent. It is as if everything has stopped around me and it's just him and me. But when he is not around and I am undergoing such rigorous penance, my mind starts questioning if my path is the right one.

My ¹*sakhis* come and taunt me about what I am doing with my life. My parents worry that I am ruining my life. My sisters remind me there is no future in what I am seeking and that I will gain nothing.my father the King is so upset with me. So the conflict exists Guruji. It's as if I am standing alone in my knowingness and everyone seems to think I am incorrect. Please help me get some clarity!"

Guruji, put his powerful hand on her head to bless her and asked, "My child, amidst all this questioning, what is your inner cognizance, your truth?" Shakti replied, "Guruji, sleeping, waking, in my dreams, amidst my chores, walking, talking, I always see my Shiva; I cannot separate myself from him. As if I am a part of him and he of me. It's as if I am his mirror and he of me. It's as if I am lifeless without him and he would probably be so without me. But Guruji, he doesn't seem to care. He is meditating and at peace in the mountains, blissfully oblivious to my yearning. It seems as if I am running after an illusion and not the truth. When I step into

¹*Sakhis - Friend

my reality here then I feel as if these things are hallucinations and there is no truth except my princess life. Please guide me. Sometimes I feel I will break down and sometimes I get so much strength that I feel I can walk towards my goals.

Guruji said, "Dear child, you have taken birth for a reason. You are not a common woman. You are Shakti. Follow your heart to your Shiva. By facing these ordeals you are helping the collective consciousness of the people to evolve. You are setting an example for the women of the world to follow. You are their Maa Durga and you are their Maa Kali. You are their Maa Laxmi and you are their Maa Saraswati. You manifest yourself in so many forms to help mankind. Your choices will help people understand their Dharma. You are the paragon for souls who need nourishment to evolve."

Saying this, the sage walked away. Not fully understanding what he meant but trying to assimilate it, Sati *(Shakti)* also moved on to her spot in the forest under the tree to meditate on the name of Shiva.

She only knew one thing and that was her goal to be with Shiva and nothing else mattered, as if the universe kept guiding her to that one goal. And she had to just follow the signs shown to her and take help when it came. The blessing of the Guruji was an invisible force that gave her strength to walk the path again. The universe always helped those on their soul path and they were never truly alone.

Chapter 21

Nandi asked Shiva, "Mahadeva, you, Lord Vishnu and Lord Brahma are all one. You are the Tridev. Then why have you all manifested in different forms. What is the divine purpose of this?" Mahadev smiled and told Nandi, "Nandi, you have become very observant. How did you even come to know we are one and same? We are just different aspects of the same energy from which our counterparts, the Devis - Maa Kali, Maa Laxmi and Maa Saraswati - are also manifested. We have divided ourselves into so many parts to manifest this universe and play the game of ¹*leela*. Now you will ask why am I playing this leela. It is this game that helps me in the evolution of my own soul energy and we keep merging back into one and dividing into different parts and then each of us again manifests and divides further until we have strands in the form of human souls separating and falling on to the earth to experience the finite birth and then merge back into us. The goal

¹*Leela - Game of illusion

of a human is to take birth, evolve and return to us. So he strives for moksha. The only way to achieve that is to move from darkness to light."

Nandi folded his hands in 2*pranama* and further asked, "What is the role of the Devis in this cycle?" Shiva explained, "The Devis are the separation of the feminine aspect from me. When we merge back, we are one again. A whole and complete soul that keeps evolving. Shakti is an integral part of me. I cannot exist without her. I make her my extension an And she too divides into many different parts to play her role in this shrishti. It is very important to understand that we are one and ultimately from the same soul essence/ Light. We have separated only for mankind to evolve and grow and expand. Can you hear the heartbeat of the universe? It is the two of us beating as ONE. I am her, she is me and we are one and the same."

2*Pranama - Salutation

Shiva went on to further explain to Nandi, "Brahma, Vishnu and I are the same and again as Brahma evolves to the Vishnu level, Vishnu will rise to the Shiva level and Shiva will rise one step further. So the game of evolution goes on at a continuous continuum. Everything has to palpitate at a certain vibration to exist. So we all exist as breaths which you and all of mankind breathe and it's constantly changing and evolving creating a life force and manifesting as the energy which merges back into us and creates another cycle. It's called the never ending cycle of life. Brahma creates, Vishnu preserves and I destroy to be created once more and the constant game of illusion goes on and on to create new truths and new realities."

Nandi prostrated before Shiva, realizing as he did so that he had also automatically done his pranama to Maa Shakti also. He also understood how the game of leela created new truths and formed new dimensions of reality. He felt exhilarated.

SHIVSHAKTI

Chapter 22

ShivShakti is an energy consciousness vibrating in the highest dimension. Mount Kailash is the main center of the receiver of this energy on Mother Earth. The energy is divided and subdivided into different forms. They co-exist to create love energy to run the universe.

Shiva and Shakti were sitting on a swing, watching the full moon and romancing. Their energies were so dynamic that they released sparks of energy that seemed like a thousand crackers lighting up the sky. Such is the energy dynamics of these two Beloveds. The sparks seemed like lightning when seen from the earth. Their energies are so mystic and volatile that they can light up the whole universe. The moonlight falling on them seemed like eternal love was glowing in the darkness of the night. The [1]*Devas* and [2]*Devis* rejoiced in the union of Shivshakti and everyone received this energy as it was distributed to the entire universe to energize and

[1]*Devas* - Gods
[2]*Devis* - Goddesses

heal. The lovers were enchanted with each other and did not have any conscious understanding of their surroundings. The whole universe seemed to one with their union. The stars in the cosmos seemed to be rejoicing and making the best of the energy available to them. The fountain of love overflowed from them to the whole of humanity.

The next morning they were visited by Lord Brahma who asked them, "Pranam! Shiva and Mother! I wonder if you realize the intensity of your union. It is like an earthquake and a volcano put together energizing all to their core and raising the vibrations of the earth. What's your purpose in doing so?"

Shiva replied as Shakti looked down coyly, "Dear Brahmadev, do you realize that all creation is thriving on our energy and it is important to energize it from time to time. I am the destroyer and I am the creator and I am the preserver. I am the very center of the universe and its movement.

It is my union with Shakti that created this beautiful world. And it is this union that energizes it and keeps it going. You are the creator but you create through me. Your creativity and Devi Saraswati's wisdom are together needed to create a new wonder, a new breath, a new life. If Shakti and I are the heart that pumps in the entire universe, you two are the womb of the earth out of which the love that exists gives form to its creation. In the same way, it is Vishnu Dev as a preserver and Maa Laxmi's abundance that balances this shrishti and keeps it going. The two of them are the roots of this shrishti and they keep it balanced and moving. It is all in synchronicity with each other. Nothing can exist without each other. Nothing at all."

Shiva was smiling and Brahma understood that he explained this to make him understand the dynamics of love, how they differed at each level. Shiva and Shakti love would be different from the very love of Brahma and Saraswati as the purpose of their togetherness was different.

Brahmadev went back to his abode smiling and happy, with a better understanding of how vital to creation and sustenance Shiva and Shakti's explosive union was.

Chapter 23

Shiva was walking around his abode and he suddenly saw a bright light in the sky. He looked towards it and saw a beautiful Angel emerging from it. He was mesmerized by her beauty.

He asked her, "Who are you?" She landed in his abode and did 1*pranama*. She said, "Oh Father of this 2*shrishti* please accept my salutations. I am an Angel and have come to ask you something." Shiva accepted her salutations and asked her to continue. She continued, "Father, why does there have to be a masculine and feminine on Earth? Why can't there be just one energy that has both together like us. We Angels are not either male or female. We are androgynous with both sexes amalgamated. We can take any gender as needed to be just like you and mother as Ardhanarishwara. So why do humans need to be one particular gender?"

1*Pranama - Salutations
2*Shristi - Universe

Shiva smiled at the angels purity and inquisitiveness and explained, "The soul is also androgynous. It is neither male nor female. But when it comes to the earth as a human birth to experience a life there, it needs to take a form as a male or a female. As life on earth is three dimensional and everything has duality, so the split is important. That's why even I, Ardhanarishwara, am divided into two for worship. It is mandatory, as in the illusion of duality that everything has an equal opposite. Hot has cold, night has day, summer has winter, man has woman, good has bad, up has down, happiness has sadness, health has sickness, and so on. It is the illusion of life, the illusion of time and space created on earth to live a life in accordance with the laws of the earth. But the earth too is now shifting to a fifth dimension and the vibrations are rising. Look down on the earth oh beautiful angel, see now people are slowly accepting a man loving a man, a woman loving a woman. Slowly the duality is fading. It is allowing higher realities to thrive amidst them. Earlier anything out of the ordinary was rejected in the name of culture and tradition. There was rigidity in structures of religion and traditions. But now so many patterns are breaking and a new earth is being created which is more tolerant of a lot of higher truths, new concepts rather than being stuck in duality. There will be less pain and suffering when the patterns break as humans will be more flexible and able to see and accept the higher or different truths. They are transcending and awakening slowly. It's a transition of the old to the new. A new path is being paved. There is a healing and clearing happening at astral, ancestral and vibration level. New levels of consciousness are being reached by the inhabitants of the earth. Soon the duality will seem a thing of the past and many illusions will be broken. Await the new earth where Shivshakti will be seen as one and not two separate forces. Just one reality, one truth!"

The divine angel smiled feeling deep gratitude for Shiva]s patience and eagerness to explain to her, she bowed down to the Jagatpita, Paramatma and got ready to leave the abode of Ardhanarishwara.

Opening her wings, the angel flew back to her realm with a deeper understanding of the concept of duality and human consciousness so she could help them better. She also understood she was not going to get caught in the duality of the earth. She would be more focused on her work and not from the space of limited viewing.

Chapter 24

There is complete perfection in creation. There is a sacred geometry in every inch of creation. If you notice the way the world is constructed, the perfection in everything How a leaf is formed, the anatomy of a tree, the complexity of the human body, the sunrise and moonrise, the galaxy and the minutest cell in a human body, all have a perfect sacred geometry. It is all a representation of the Shivshakti energy that it consists of.

The dynamics of this energy that forms the minutest particle in this galaxy is flawless. When one prays to the Shivalingam, one usually just offers milk to it and prays for one's desire to be fulfilled. But has one understood what we are supposed to do when we pray to a Shivalingam has a deeper meaning and method to it.

A Shivalingam is a union of Shivashakti, a merger of the masculine and feminine genders. For anything to manifest, for any prayer to be heard, it has to be created from an Ardhanarishwara. That is, only when the two parts are whole can they create anew. So when you create, it is important to integrate your logic and intuition (masculine and feminine) even within yourself and you are sure to gain success. When you worship the Shivalingam, it is important to understand what it stands for. There is a snake coiled three and a half times around the lingam. It represents the Kundalini Shakti which resides in each one of us in our [1]*Mooladhara Chakra* and it is the Kundalini Shakti within that one must work on while meditating on the lingam.

As you meditate on the Shivalingam, i.e. the consciousness of Ardhanarishwara, you can raise your Kundalini and attain spiritual enlightenment. That is the main purpose of the Shivalingam and not just fulfilling desires. It is the divine energy of the Shivalingam that can take you across the seven [2]*chakras* into

[1]*Mooladhara Chakra - Root Chakra
[2]*Chakras - Realms

the abode of Shivshakti in ³*Kailash where it blooms into a thousand-petalled lotus. It awakens your Kundalini and your masculine and feminine flow into each other in perfect harmony, making you a balanced energy body.

The true purpose of the Shivalingam is to provide enlightenment and help you unite with your own inner Ardhanarishwara.

³*Kailash - Crown Chakra

SHIVSHAKTI

Chapter 25

Once, after an argument due to a difference of opinion with Shiva, Shakti left their abode and went away to her parent's home. She was so upset with Shiva, she couldn't handle her anger. She was pacing up and down the lawn of her father's palace in anger when her mother, the Queen, came up to her and asked, "My dear ¹*Putri*, what makes you so angry? Why are you like a volcano about to burst? Your anger will burn the ²*prithvi*, please gain control over it. And pray tell me what's the reason for so much emotion for a Devi like you who is so evolved and doesn't get angry quickly."

Shakti stopped in her tracks and bowing down to her mother, replied, "Mother, I am a very gentle and loving woman. My love is very giving and unconditional. I am also very patient. But when every limit is crossed, then my rage is as powerful as my silence and patience. Shiva and I had an argument, mother. In our differences of opinion I have to once again be the one to

¹*Putri - Daughter
²*Prithvi - Earth

understand, compromise or forget that my opinion may be the correct one and I too have a right to be heard. Just because he is the masculine aspect and my husband doesn't entitle him to behave like my owner. My rage is at my emotions and opinions not being acknowledged. Shiva seems to sit in his meditation so blissfully that it shakes me even more and I wonder if I am not as evolved as him. He seems so evolved that in 3*_dhyana_, he is able to disregard the argument between us and obtain bliss. And that makes me angrier till I am finally in a rage. I feel disrespected that my views remain unheard or ignored. Where am I wrong, Mother? Why is a female always supposed to understand and compromise?"

Her mother heard her woes with a lot of patience allowing Shakti to vent and first hugged her child to calm her and then sat her down. She explained to Shakti, "Shakti you are Jagat Mata, the epitome of unconditional love. A mother is the highest position anyone can ever hold. You are Jagat Mata, you are the veritable acme of love. And always remember, the masculine and feminine

3*Dhyana - Meditation

have opposing and complementary aspects. That's why energy is divided into two. So, while you have the quality of being able to compromise, Shiva has the authority factor in him. Sometimes they clash and it leads to conflict. There might be a difference of opinion and you might feel that you are not being heard. It is very momentary. Remember other times when he has accorded your opinions respect and treated you with utmost regard. When he has heard you out and acted on your advice. Remember he always allows you your space. Now too he is allowing you to feel your emotions fully and vent them. He has a right to stick to his point of view and if he doesn't not understand your point of view for some reason, remember that you as his [4]*ardhangini* also need to give him space and allowance. Your allowance will give him the room to think and on his own he will understand your point of view. But you need to feel secure and at peace with yourself meanwhile. He can take his time about it and you cannot hurry him. It's his own mind mapping which will be used at his level of

[4]*Ardhangini - The better half

understanding to assimilate what you have told him. Who knows what you felt was rejection while he went to sit on his asana, can be him actually wanting to ponder over what you told him. What you took it as his coldness and rejection and what made you seethe in anger may actually have been him trying to understand you. He could be wrong in the way he went about it but not in his intentions. Always see what the purity of the intention behind someone's action is and you shall always be happy and calm" So saying, her mother stroked Shakti's head lovingly and embraced her once again. Shakti saw that she had reacted in ego and her own understanding of the situation had increased the conflict between her and her prannath. She calmed down and bowed to her mother and the sky and the five elements.

The five elements around her were holding her while she went through the transformation from ego into wisdom and in deep gratitude headed back to her home.

Chapter 26

Maa Shakti is the embodiment of the feminine aspect of life. She shows the different manifestations of a woman. As Parvati she is an [1]*Ardhangini*, a faithful wife who is the other half as Shiva. As Durga she is an example of how a woman is [2]*paripoorna* in herself and doesn't need any man's support. She represents strength, valour and independence. As Laxmi, she portrays the womanly qualities of grace and abundance. She represents the importance of fulfilling earthly desires. As Saraswati, she portrays knowledge and wisdom. She represents culture, innocence and music. As Kali, she is the fiercest of all and this roopa is needed to face the strongest of enemies and. Radha is the epitome of unconditional love even in separation. She and her beloved are revered together even though they never undergo the sacred ties of marriage. Can anyone dare point at Radha and say she is having an affair?

[1]*Ardhangini - The better half
[2]*Paripoorna - complete

Shakti has divided herself into these manifestations to make humanity understand her different aspects as well as those of Shiva, love, and union. Look at Meera, she is another form of Shakti, representing the quality of Devotion. She is portrayed as a human being to make people understand that love for God/ the Beloved doesn't change irrespective of the forms you take. She takes separation, unity, devotion to another level. Shakti has further divided herself into kuldevis. She has many more ³*roopas and in every aspect she portrays a different version of herself. Is she a different person? No!! She is the same energy in different forms and if you are able to cut through the illusion of forms, you will see Shakti herself everywhere, in all these different versions. They are just different representations which take you back to the same Shiva.

³*Roopas - Personalties

Even in all her forms you cannot miss Shiva. He exists within her always. He exists as Vishnu, Rama, Krishna, Brahma and many other masculine versions to match feminine strength and power His versions also vary in their personality traits to portray an equal and opposite version of her energy display. They are equal, respectful, opposite, magnetic, energies. They manifest as equal and complimentary opposites to complete the circle of life. They require each other to be complete and yet are complete in their own way. It's a game of life manifesting in and out of different levels of consciousness in different forms and all are one at the same time. They are and they are not at the same moment. The eternal dance of the Shivshakti manifests itself in various forms.

Shivshakti dance to each other tunes in perfect harmony, satisfying each other's needs, moods, desires, and strengths with eagerness and the devotion of love.

SHIVSHAKTI

Chapter 27

Kailasa, the abode of Shiva. It is the dream of every devotee of Shiva to visit it at least once in a lifetime. It is an energy portal to the other dimensions. There are multiple portals of various levels there, and energies enter and exit these portals inter-dimensionally. It is a space created by the creator for the energies to enter the earth. Shiva residing here is an energy of the highest intensity, sending these energies down to the earth where there are many natural and manmade antennas to receive and broadcast these energies widely.

Shiva is a symbol of magnificent grandeur, an ever graceful symbol of fatherhood. Let us compare Lord Vishnu's energies to Shiva's. Shiva is very powerful, with a strong muscular body adorned with Rudrakshas and a snake and wearing just a cloth around his waist. He controls the moon and River Ganga and of course the snake Vasuki around his neck. He sports a powerful weapon, the *Trishul* and holds a *Damroo*. He portrays an image of simplicity, of someone who has overcome all his fears, wants and needs. No one can challenge him as he is the master of all.

Lord Vishnu has a more gentle energy. He is more feminine energy to his masculine and he emits it as love energy. He wears rich garments and is adorned with jewelry and a crown. His majestic appearance is that of an abundant king. He always carries a discus, a mace and a conch. He has taken many births on earth in different forms such as Krishna, Rama, Parsurama etc. to teach mankind new ways to live and help them build social systems. He ruled over three yugas the *Satyuga*, *Dwaparayuga* and *Tretayuga* and he helped humanity achieve shifts in its consciousness. He has already come down to the earth in nine avatars and one is still pending when we reach the Golden Aquarian age when he will come once again to help humanity raise its consciousness

Shiva remains in Kailasa aiding mankind from there. The abode of Shiva is an entire realm and not just a mountain. It has doorways to different worlds. Shiva controls all aspects of the universe, the entire galactic system and the cosmos. Shiva sends Shakti and Vishnu to the earth to raise the consciousness of humanity. Vishnu's gentle energies are more conducive to the planet and he is able to hold space in the Earth's dimensions. Shiva's energies are so powerful that they will destroy the earth if he comes as an avatar. Such power is needed to run the entire universe which he does sitting in Kailasa. But in reality they are not different. They are one and the same. Vishnu just carries more of Shakti within him and is a gentler form of Shiva so that he can come to the earth and help balance everything. He is just a different form of the same Shivshakti.

That's why we say God is one, just has different forms. The energy shifts in consciousness to manifest itself to play the leela for mankind.

ANITA RAJANI

SHIVSHAKTI

Chapter 28

Separation is always difficult. Distance can be due to many reasons which are beyond the control of the two people involved.

Silence is very powerful!!!!

During one such time, Krishna *(Shiva)* shut himself down to avoid any drama, a typical masculine way to cope up with the situation. As he wanted to maintain harmony and to keep peace around him, he withdrew his energies and became silent. Radha *(Shakti)* had a different way of coping with the separation. She was getting restless and sad. The separation was taking her spiraling down into negative emotions. She felt it was the end of the world. How would she cope? Why was the world so insensitive to love? Didn't she just love her Kanha? Her love was her devotion and it came from the purest aspect of her soul and yet she was forbidden to meet her Beloved. She was angry and upset. Her [1]*sakhi* was sitting

[1]*Sakhi - Friend

with her and consoling her as she could empathize with her pain. She was allowing her to vent.

Radha *(Shakti)* told her sakhi, "Looking at my Kanha, I lose my senses and feel as if there are butterflies in my stomach. I am overpowered by the love between us. I get blinded by his presence and it is as if time stops and there is no one around. Only my beloved and me. It's the most magical moment. Hearing him playing his flute I leave everything and without caring about the world and its barriers I run to him. I am in awe of him. He is the very essence of my life, my breath. Without him, I cannot survive. How am I going to cope with this separation? Why is his family against me and wanting him to leave me from attending to his duties? Am I non-existent, don't I matter? My love is true."

Her sakhi replied, "Radhe, no one here understands love. Everyone is consumed by ifs and buts and dos and don'ts. Logic rules the mind. The heart has no place. Your love will be recognized by the whole world when the time comes, but not right now." Radha

Radha *(Shakti)* begins to weep, her mind spirals into worry about the future of her love for Krishna *(Shiva)*. She is consumed by her fears and anxiety. She says, "Sakhi, I wonder why Kanha is silent, doesn't he miss me? Doesn't he feel he has a dharma towards me also? Just because I cannot marry him, does this make my love less eligible? His shutting down makes me wonder what he is going through."

Krishna *(Shiva)* was silently pacing up and down his room in his palace, wondering, "How can I honor my love to Radhe? There has to be a way. There must be a way. Why is my dharma to my kingdom and why don't the people or culture allow Radhe to be by my side? How do I honor her? Radhe exists in my every breath and she is my Shakti. Why am I supposed to abandon her because she doesn't fit the image of an ideal wife for me? She is so in me and I in her. My life force will not retain its balance if she doesn't exist. I have to find a way."

But the moment a guard came to call Krishna *(Shiva)* to the courtyard as everyone was waiting for the meeting, he quickly recovered from his trauma of separation. He knew his services were needed by the people of his kingdom to help them clear their karma. It was his sole purpose for coming down into the world.

Somewhere both were worrying and anxious about each other but not able to communicate their emotions of separation. There was so much silence which could be heard by all who could see the separation of Shivshakti for the purpose of the upliftment of the souls of the people of Dwapara Yuga!!!

Chapter 29

Separation is a testing time. Every relationship goes through ups and downs and the down times test how much you love each other and how much you can endure and still choose each other!!

Krishna *(Shiva)* was married to Rukmini and busy with his kingdom. He was following the path of his dharma. He was an incarnation doing his duty. One day Radha *(Shakti)* came to Dwarka to meet Krishna *(Shiva)*. When they met, their eyes locked and the whole past of their relationship of love was recreated in front of their eyes. They sat together for hours. In silence, as being together completed them in many ways. They were [1]*paripoorna* together. They communicated through their silence and their breaths. The pain of separation melted for a while and they became whole again.

[1]*Paripoorna - Complete

Radha *(Shakti)* asked Krishna *(Shiva)*, "Can I stay in the palace as one of the devikas and serve you. At least I will see you everyday and my pain will lessen." Krishna *(Shiva)* agreed and allotted her a place in the palace. She began to serve him, but something was amiss. She didn't see the Krishna *(Shiva)* she knew. He was a different person. He had changed. Her Kanha was a humble shepherd who was playful and innocent. In his place was a serious king who served his people. Something had died inside him. She realized that just as she was not alive without him, he too was a living corpse without his Radha *(Shakti)*. He had also has lost the childlike charm that he had in Gokul. She understood that just as she had suffered, he too had suffered but being a divine masculine he did not express it as freely as her. He held it all in, his pain and suffering. She was at peace and at the same time sad. She didn't think she could survive seeing her Kanha this way. In her thoughts, she walked out of the palace and walked towards the forest. Krishna *(Shiva)* saw her and followed her.

He called her name but she didn't hear and kept walking in deep trauma until she reached a place deep in the forest. She sat down by a tree sad and dejected.

Krishna *(Shiva)* asked her, "Radhe, why are you looking so lost? Please tell me. How can I help you?" Radha *(Shakti)* looked at Krishna *(Shiva)* and said, "I am lost since the day we separated, my Beloved. It is as if there is no life force left in me. I have come to you, drawn like a magnet but you too seem lost. You don't say anything but I see it all. I see it in your eyes Kanha." Tears welled up in the eyes of both. Krishna *(Shiva)* still didn't express much of what he felt. He knew Radha *(Shakti)* understood his silence. He didn't need to put it in words. Radha *(Shakti)* asked him to play his flute and Krishna *(Shiva)* obliged. He played and played and released all his pain and suffering in the ²*dhun that blew out of the flute.

Radha *(Shakti)* slowly kept releasing her pain and suffering and merged with the music of the flute and her Kanha's essence. As the

²*Dhun - Tune

flute played and the music filled the entire forest, she released herself from her physical body and ended her life in the *Dwaparayuga*. She was finally at peace as the physical body gave her pain of separation and in the soul world she was always with Kanha. She didn't need to be in pain. After a while, Krishna *(Shiva)* wiped his tears and stopped playing the flute. He saw Radha's *(Shakti)* 3*shava* lying on the ground. But he knew she had merged with his essence and now they were one. He also no longer felt pain. She took all his pain with her so he could perform his dharma without any conflict and bring glory to his kingdom and achieve his soul's purpose. Now she would always reside in him and he was Shivshakti. He went back from the forest paripoorna and equipped to successfully deal with the challenges before him. He was not happy but neither was he sad. He just felt complete and one with his Radha *(Shakti)*.

Now the world could see him as Shivashakti and they had only one name on their lips "Radhakrishna Radhakrishna!!"

3*Shava - Dead Body

"Radhakrishna...RadhaKrishna..."

Chants in the air....

Krishna playing the flute, Radha dancing,

Gopis in the background, exotic and divine.

Humming the music as the soul dances and feels entwined.

Singing the song of love, which seems endless, egoless,

a state of pure beingness with complete surrender

And complete nothingness, the Kundalinis merging.

"Radhe Radhe" Krishna calls.

Radhe runs to him blinded with love

Feels the instant electric connection

Gets lost in the ecstasy of love the merger, the union.

Oblivious of the surroundings,

In complete ecstasy of being with her Beloved.

A knowingness of you and me!

ANITA RAJANI

The dance of Radha, as Krishna plays the flute is like the millions of stars dancing,

Krishna seems mesmerized by Radha's eyes and her body dancing to his music.

Lost in love's glory, seemingly a new story,

To know, to merge with the Beloved

To reach the divine and create magic for all...

The universe plays a melody of love!!

Butterflies all around, birds singing, clouds dancing, water drops glowing in the sunshine, rivers gushing, forests enchanting, green grass shining, each feeling the love, the love between Radha Krishna as if acknowledging that nothing else exists, but the divine truth that is 'LOVE'!!

Chapter 30

Shiva's silence was very loud. The longer the period of separation, the clearer his unspoken words and the meaning of his actions in Shakti's mind. She understood why he had behaved the way he had so often when she felt that he didn't even care. She now realized that he too had the fear of losing her just as she had and that he too felt miserable in the separation but that these separation periods were very important for growth at all levels of consciousness. They seemed full of pain but the process was actually bringing about transformation in the mind, body and spirit and the evolution of the collective consciousness of mankind. It was working at multidimensional levels and bringing about changes in behavior, thoughts, conditioning, past patterns and karmic cycles. It seemed like a punishment but was actually a healing space, a blessing in disguise.

Hundreds of years pass by creating the right consciousness of love for mankind to dwell on. It is not simple to create a pool of unconditional love. It is not by chance that we can access the realm of love. It has been created through lots of energy transformation of Shivshakti in various forms and at different levels of learning. It is a churning like the Samudra Manthan where the vish is separated from the Amrut. More than the amrut itself, it is the process of churning, the discomfort, and that of forming an inner peace that is important. It is only Shiva who can drink the vish; only he has the capacity to achieve the greatest of great things. He seems to just sit and meditate in silence but he is actually building up the energy to create and recreate this kind of magnanimous energy.

Shakti was able to perceive this magnanimity of Shiva. He seemed to be silent and inactive but his presence itself made a difference. She felt she was the doer in the relationship and the one directing but she understood how much he too contributed without wanting to take credit. Shakti realized she had a slight feeling that she was the better partner and working harder to make things work between them but that it was a two-way process and nothing happened through her efforts alone. Shiva's efforts may be subtle enough to pass unnoticed but she understood that his efforts were as important as hers and her ego melted and the lotus of her heart chakra opened up more and more to increase the quotient of unconditional love within her. She was ready to dive deeper within her own consciousness and clear her shadows which were causing barriers in the smooth flow of the relationship. No longer did she blame only Shiva for their love tiffs and understood how her darkness too played a role in the entire relationship dynamics. Who knew what further clarity would surface in this separation period?

She thought to herself maybe Shiva was also facing his own shadows and evolving further. After all he was the epitome of male consciousness and he also had a responsibility to keep evolving like she had.

It didn't seem like separation anymore, just a healing time. Everything could suddenly be perceived as an illusion. The pain was slowly vanishing allowing only love to thrive!!!

Chapter 31

Rama *(Shiva)* saw the princess and instantly their eyes met. Everyone in the kingdom knew she was not born of the Queen. She had been found in a burrow and was known as the daughter of Mother Earth. She was not a human birth but a consciousness known as Sita *(Shakti)*. As soon as they saw each other, the knowingness of the soul came flashing back to both of them and their eyes locked. They both remembered their souls were twins and they needed no introduction. They were born for a higher purpose and had come to fulfill that purpose. Nothing could come between their love of a thousand lifetimes manifested in this birth as the love of Rama *(Shiva)* and Sita *(Shakti)*. They both understood that their journey would begin together again now as each other's better halves or as Ardhanaishwara.

Rama *(Shiva)* won Sita *(Shakti)*, vanquishing many other eligible bachelors as destiny was with them. The beautiful, graceful damsel whom he saw and recognized as his beloved was finally his. He felt elated and joyful. He was the most eligible bachelor and she was the most beautiful princess. It was a typical fairytale full of magic and glamour and their wedding was the most lavish and splendid ever even among royals. It was the most beautiful celestial wedding ever seen, as if the stars danced and the skies rejoiced in their union.

When they become the target of people's jealousy and wrath, they did not give up on their love. The love always remained intact. As a couple, they were interdependent and very supportive of each other. The perfect example of how the two energies can blend in the perfect mix to create love, righteousness, values and beliefs. He respected her and was always in awe of her providing all she wanted. She was the happiest of wives, serving her husband as expected of a princess of *Satya Yuga*.

Truth prevailed in the *Satya Yuga* and the truth of love spread over the entire land of Ayodhya. But alas, the dream did not last long as human jealousy couldn't bear to see their idyllic love. The love was put to the test. When Rama *(Shiva)* was sent into exile Sita *(Shakti)* followed him like a true Beloved. They stood every test of time, serving their destiny which was a thorny one. Life was not a bed of roses and yet they endured all the pain and suffering, finding happiness and solace in each other until she was abducted by Ravana. Ravana was so mesmerized with Sita's *(Shakti)* beauty that it was fit to be in a palace rather than wasted in exile in the forest. He enticed her with all the riches in the world, testing her faithfulness. But true love cannot be enticed with material wealth or titles. It is happy to endure all pain. The richness of true love once felt cannot be discarded.

True love is equivalent to being one with God. It is a doorway to heaven and can never be traded for any material objects. Such was the love of the two beloveds of Satya Yuga!!!

Chapter 32

A divine marriage and living happily ever after happens only in fairytales. Rama *(Shiva)* and Sita *(Shakti)* could not live a magical life for very long. Envy, jealousy and betrayals soon came to the fore. When Rama *(Shiva)* was banished from the kingdom, Sita *(Shakti)* had a choice. She could choose material comforts and luxury or she could choose her love. Sita *(Shakti)* was a very wise soul and had come to the world for the sole purpose of being with her beloved. She chose love and followed her other half to the forest, knowing that it was going to be a life of hardship. But the test of love had to be undergone. They had to set an example of what true love is. She chose to walk on thorns and wear a crown of flowers rather than diamonds and gold. She set a standard for love that is talked about even thousands of years later. Her choices in her life, her sacrifices, and her life everything is from an evolved space, a space of strength, a true Shakti. Her life from being born of Mother Earth to living the childhood of a princess, marrying a king in a fairytale wedding and then having to forsake all her riches was not an easy one. Choosing rags after being used to riches is not easy.

Every step of the way she walked by the side of her beloved, proving her worthiness to him. She was the perfect partner. In return, she too had the perfect partner in all aspects. He was the perfect husband who always treated her courteously and respected her views. He kept her protected and yet gave her the freedom of choices. He never forced his views on anyone. The divine feminine and the divine masculine were in perfect sync in their union. The universe still had a series of tests for them. After living a life of such privation together she was abducted by the most powerful man to seduce her. [1]*Ravana* could not rest at peace seeing such a divine woman and wanted her to succumb to material desires. He waited for her to give in to her need for comfort and riches. Little did he realize that she had no such needs as she had discarded

[1]*Ravana* - Male Ego

them long back. Ravana would not win this battle. Sita *(Shakti)* was not going to fail her test. Her every moment was spent in remembering her Beloved and she knew that he would come to her rescue. She had the strength to hold on to her purity, keeping her lower desires in check and higher knowingness at a peak as she waited for her Beloved. She knew he would be yearning for her as she yearned for him. She was sure of their victory and the death of Ravana who had wanted to suppress the divine feminine and make her a slave to his whims and fancies in the name of giving her the riches of the world.

She didn't get entangled in the ²*Maya Jal* having a far higher vision than he could even imagine. She knew that this was a trap to test her purity, patience and love for her Beloved and she passed the test. Hanumanji came to her rescue. He flew across the challenge of the eternal ocean to tell her that her Beloved was just about to reach and not to give up hope. He protected her till Rama *(Shiva)* could reach the island. Rama *(Shiva)* was stuck at the other end of

²*Maya Jal - Web of illusion

the ocean and was helped by all his inner 3**instincts* to reach his beloved to rescue her from Ravana. They were reunited and returned in bliss to much celebration and grandeur. They thought they had passed all their tests and won the battle of love over ego. The higher consciousness had won over the lower consciousness. It had taken time but it was well worth the effort. They were welcomed back to their kingdom with as much enthusiasm and joy as they felt deep with their united hearts.

They were not the prince and princess anymore. They had come back mature and evolved to make the right choices with complete wisdom for the highest good of all. They now truly deserved and had won the title of the king and queen. They had reached their destiny!!

3*Instincts - Monkeys

Chapter 33

The beautiful love story of Rama *(Shiva)* and Sita *(Shakti)* does not end in a happy ending. Even these beings of highest vibrations when incarnated on the earth in different Yugas had to face many challenges. Then who are we mortals who have descended from the strands of Shivshakti. The evolution of different yugas can be seen clearly till humanity reached *Kali Yuga*. It is the evolution of the entire universe and Shivshakti. All are evolving at the same pace in harmony with each other.

All the three yugas had Vishnu avatars who worshipped the Shiva lingam. Shiva had to take the form of Vishnu to descend to the earth and Shakti's role to match each avatar was painful and full of suffering. Kali yuga saw the divine feminine slowly rising as Shakti had to take the form of the Kali to face the demons born out of masculine ego that were suppressing Shakti in all ages and times. She was meant to sacrifice for the sake of her duties, family, the kingdom and the divine masculine. Why was she suppressed? Why she was not allowed to retain all her power? Why was she always made to suffer? Because if the divine feminine rose to power, there would be no ills in the world, there would be no devils and demons as she is a slayer of demons that cause harm. If Shakti has to adorn the roopa of a Kali or a Durga she can win any battle over any demon and will not allow the lower energies to persist. Before she could attain such power, she was suppressed.

Kali Yuga is for the divine feminine to rise. When Shakti awakens within each one of us, her name will attain its true meaning. Each one of us needs to get empowered to kill the demonic energies of *Kali Yuga*. The combined Shivshakti is the most empowered space to be in. The right and left brain are balanced and inner harmony is maintained. Intuition and logic are in divine play with each other to create success and strength.

That space can be the goal of every human to achieve. Shivshakti will then resonate in its highest vibration across the entire universe to the sound of the word OM - which is again a Shivshakti.

Shivshakti is a breath in and a breath out. It is the same within and without. It is duality as well as oneness. It is the micro and the macro of the universe. It is the earth and the sky. It is Prakriti and Purusha. It is the sun and the moon. It is Shivshakti.

SHIVSHAKTI

Chapter 34

Rama *(Shiva)* was crowned the king. He was pacing up and down his room in his palace deep in thought. Every day, once his kingly duties were over, he would retire to his bedroom and think about Sita *(Shakti)*. He wondered if she was doing well and was worried about her health. He was sad and unhappy that he had regained his position but she was still being tested. He would have given it all up for her in that one instant but for the look in her eye. She was strong and respected herself too much to be affected by someone judging her character. For her, what her Beloved thought of her was what mattered as she knew what her own inner truth was. She was not affected by people who didn't matter to her and what their opinions about her were.

For her the love in Rama's *(Shiva)* eyes for her was more than enough. She was not craving any palaces and riches. What mattered was her togetherness with her Beloved. But that was also not possible now as being a Queen entailed going by certain rules. Carrying the love of Rama *(Shiva)* in her heart forever, she walked out of the kingdom with her head held high knowing she was pure and chaste. She didn't need to prove anything to anyone.

She had so much strength and valor that she didn't even stop to think where she would go and what she would do. She knew she would be led by the divine light as everything was an illusion. She understood that her role as Rama's wife forever by his side was over. She had been his support and strength throughout the [1]*banvas* but now being back in the kingdom he would excel and do well on his own. She knew her *role* (soul purpose) was coming to an end. She had to just give him his sons so they could follow in their father's footsteps. Bringing up Luv and Kush in an ashram, she gave, them the sanskaras of great warriors in their early childhood years. Once she had got them ready, she presented them to their father.

[1]*Banvas - Exile

Rama *(Shiva)* who had never once doubted it, flinched seeing his sons, knowing instantly they were his blood. His love for Sita *(Shakti)* was so great that he never spent a moment without her name or image next to him. He lived only because he knew that she was alive and under the same sky somewhere and that gave him the strength to run his kingdom. But he was alone in his loneliness. He had no one to share it with. He never once thought of marrying again and stayed true to Sita *(Shakti)* and her alone till his last breath. He would always feel the void with Sita *(Shakti)* not by his side.

In those times, women were not treated as the equals of men. They were supposed to be subservient to the masculine and had to follow the laws of chastity. Sita *(Shakti)* had to undergo the fire ritual as a purity test but even after passing the test was not accepted and had to leave the kingdom. Rama *(Shiva)* and Sita *(Shakti)* were much evolved energies and yet ever evolving and understanding the dynamics of their balance. The feminine were not allowed to rise and that made the masculine so restless and thereby creating a void and pain of separation which still doesn't allow them to unite now even though thousands of years have passed by. The memory imprints of the separation are so deep.

Somewhere the masculine realizes and is guilty he didn't keep her safe and he didn't give her justice. He was so bound by the collective consciousness of society that he felt his hands were bound. He is not able to forgive himself after even thousands of years and feels unfit and incapable of even loving her again. He feels he is not worthy of the love of a woman who sacrificed her all for him and went with him to the forest. And when it was time to give her happiness,

Rama *(Shiva)* didn't have the courage to stand up for the truth of his love, although he is known for his truth. It was his shadow unresolved part which still needed to evolve. The masculine needed to stand up for his love so they could together ascend to another level. Separation seemed to be the crux for love.

There is no neural pathway to believe that the world accepts true love. Everything else and everyone else always seems more important than love which should be the basis and foundation of all families.

It is time to renew the contract of true love. It is time to unite and merge. It is time for true love to thrive!!!

Chapter 35

The transient phase of Shivshakti lasted for thousands of years. It is going on from one Yuga to another. We slowly have to keep transcending and reach a state of shambhala where each person is looked upon as a human being and not a man or woman. Where unity is and complete. There are no imbalances of duality. It is a state of mind, spirit and ethereal reality where heaven and Earth are one and the kundalini is in an awakened state. But to reach there the masculine and feminine are still finding their way up. They are ascending and falling and rising again, struggling their way up. Rama *(Shiva)* was a God to his [1]*praja* as he proved to be the best king they had had but his personal space was very painful. His self-worth was low as he thought he was no longer worthy of true love as he had harmed his own [2]*Ardhangini* and not proved to be a good husband. His name and fame didn't mean anything to him in comparison.

[1]*Praja - People of his kingdom
[2]*Ardhangini - The better half

Sita *(Shakti)* at the same time showed strength of steel, facing adversity all alone. She was an example of true woman power that cannot be broken. The world could go against her and she was capable of facing all the trials alone. She didn't need to be with a man to prove her self-worth. She didn't for a minute allow her self-esteem to fall or be overcome with shame. Her purity was her weapon. Her belief in self was her shield. She was Kali, Durga, Laxmi all rolled into one. She was always 'The Awakened'. She didn't need to awaken. She was always balanced and didn't need to seek stability. So also in the collective consciousness, the feminine is mostly awakened while the masculine struggles with shame and low self-worth. The masculine may have lost its way as it is nothing without Shakti.

Sita *(Shakti)* had to finally end her life and surrender to [2]*Prithvi Mata* as the she could unite with Rama *(Shiva)* in the ethereal world and he too would not have to rule the kingdom carrying the pain of separation from his Beloved in his heart. She would now

[2]*Prithvi Mata - Mother Earth

exist within him and make him complete in a way - paripoorna - so he could focus on his soul purpose of ruling humanity and teaching them values of truth, honesty, strength and unconditional love. The pain that he carried in his heart finally broke his heart into a million pieces, allowing the light to enter. It transformed his pain for Sita *(Shakti)* into unconditional love for the whole of humanity and he thus became the greatest king known to man.

Rama (Shiva) was now evolved into a divine masculine who could handle situations with ease as his heart and mind were in complete balance. He was SitaRam - the male who followed the female giving her due for her sacrifice and love for him.

Chapter 36

Shiva and Shakti were running around in the mountains, mischief in their eyes, their laughter echoing in the valleys. The ¹*ghungroos on Shakti's feet sounded like bells ringing and energizing the universe. Shiva and Shakti's light-hearted playful mood was a sight to fill the heart with joy. It left a wonderful imprint of happiness and bliss. It spread the feeling of oneness and love, of hope and light. The warmth that it radiated can only be felt and not expressed in words. At last, they sat down on the cliff with their feet hanging down towards the valley.

They smiled with contentment as they watched the sun set. Shakti asked Shiva, "Prannath, why is it that when ²*Shrishti emerged from Brahma's ³*nabhi the first humans appeared on the earth all were treated equal. Women were treated as equals of men and honoured for who they were. What happened along the way? How did the masculine overpower them? Why did society begin to downgrade

¹* Ghungroos - Trinklets
²*Shristi - Universe
³*Nabhi - Navel

women into suppressing their qualities and creativity, restricting them within the boundaries of the home? How did males learn to objectify them? Why did rapes begin and how did the masculine become so insensitive that he forgot the feminine was an aspect of me and when she assumed the Kali roopa, no one could touch her? How and why? I want to know. It enrages me to see women being pushed around and told that they are not worthy and need to be just bound to their homes. When did it become unsafe for women to walk alone, live alone, and work for their living? I am puzzled at what's happening on Earth."

Shiva explained, "Shakti, I will share a secret with you: a man is a weakling, he appears very strong and powerful but actually he is very weak when he is without his feminine aspect. His fear that the feminine will be strong and not need him and he will end up being the second gender, ruffle's his ego so much that he does everything under his power to keep control. He tries to clip her wings so she cannot fly high. He crushes her self-esteem so much that she forgets she is Shakti. She gets so blinded by the illusions of low self-worth, and inability to be independent that the masculine dominates. Once the illusion breaks and the feminine realizes that she is the ultimate power and has been kept under suppression, do you know what will happen?"

Shakti asks, "No, please tell me, Prannath". He stands up on the edge of a cliff, looks at the vast blue sky and opens his arms, says, "Shakti will rise from the ashes like the Phoenix and run the world. She is the mother of the universe and every woman will represent that. She will be compassionate and at the same time strong. She will be gentle and at the same time very assertive. She will be the nurturer and at the same time Kali. She will be as open and as vast as this sky but when it thunders everyone views it with respect. No one can move without the sky showering its grace and everyone bows to it in acknowledgement. Such will be the essence of every woman on earth. Then she will not be burnt for dowry or banished for being impure. She will rule the home and everyone will respect her values and her demeanor. She will be Maa Shakti and I, Shiva, bow down to the essence of Maa Shakti, which is you my beloved.

Shakti smiled, knowing that this collective consciousness of the feminine is rising slowly and one day it will rise high enough to merge with her. Shiva and she turned around and walked back to their beautiful abode.

Chapter 37

Sati *(Shakti)* was walking along the beach, sad and depressed and yearning for her Shiva. She was wondering why she had to go through so much yearning and separation to unite with Shiva. She was strolling in the dark of the night with the moonlight shining on the edges of the waves making beautiful twinkling lights in the water. She was blankly staring at the sea water and the waves lashing at the banks.

Just then Brahma appeared and she immediately bowed down to him. He asked her, "Sati *(Shakti)* , why are you so upset. What are you thinking of?"

Sati replied, "I am wondering how to reach my Shiva. Why is it taking so long? I am doing everything I can to reduce my karmic burden and make my way to my Shiva, but the challenges don't seem to end. One after the other, they are hurled at me and sometimes I feel it is impossible that I can reach him. He seems so far away, always silent, happy where he is. And I seem always to be struggling with my memories and images of him which makes it impossible to be happy and content where I am. My goals don't let me sleep. I keep staring at the moon and see only my Shiva in it."

Brahma pointed his finger at the edge of the sea and thousands of Shivalingas popped up in the water. They were a sight to behold and the sea water lashed at them so that only their tops can be seen. It seemed magical, like the water was embracing the lingams.

Feeling ecstatic she ran towards them. Brahma smiled and said, "These lingams will take you close to your Shiva. Until then embrace them and do their seva, so you can clear your penance period. Do the needful, so your journey to your Shiva is finally over. It is very important to know that he is with you always. Although he seems [1]*magna*, his wait is as significant as yours. He leads you to him. He pulls you towards him. It is his magnetic aura that keeps you thinking of him always. It is he who is actually

---

[1]*Magna - Lost in a trance

more restless than you. It may seem you are doing the penance alone but he is aiding you and ensuring that you do not leave him or stop thinking about him. He wants you as much as you want him.

Brahma left and she walked towards the sea, putting her feet in the cold water and finally touching the lingams. The moment she touched one lingam her memories of being together with her Shiva came flooding back and she was lost in a trance. She began serving the lingams and clearing her karma.

Her separation from her Beloved no longer seemed like a punishment. She realized that 'what you seek, seeks you too. And it was only a matter of time when her Shiva will come seeking her!!!'

Chapter 38

Radha *(Shakti)* was sitting in the front yard of the palace taking a break from her work in the palace. She watched Rukmini laughing and strolling in the yard. She wondered why she was the privileged one to marry Krishna *(Shiva)* and why she, despite being Krishna's *(Shiva)* Beloved, still had to long for him. Was this fair to her? What kind of karma did she have to see Krishna and never be his? And Rukmini, on the other hand, became his wife without even yearning for him.

Hearing her thoughts, with due respect to Shakti, Lord Vishnu came to her and told her, "Radha *(Shakti)*, I was hearing you thinking about your destiny with Krishna *(Shiva)*. You are his Shakti and you know that." Radha *(Shakti)* said, "Yes Deva but why am I born older, why are we having so many problems that we can't marry and be together. What's the purpose of my birth if I have to stay away from my beloved?"

Lord Vishnu replied, "The purpose of your birth is not to live a happy life with Krishna *(Shiva)*. You have a much larger purpose. Your essence is one with Shiva and no one can separate it. Even though he is married to Rukmini, everyone will worship you as his Beloved and only you two will be seen together not Rukmini. That is the law of the universe and your destiny. The purpose of your life is not in the physical dimension but in the ethereal dimension. Your being married to someone else does not take away the purity of your love. How can love be impure? How can you be the other woman, or the hidden one? You are the very essence of Krishna *(Shiva)* and that's what humanity has to learn, that love is pure and love is just love. It cannot be anything else. Love can be layered, with many layers of negative beliefs and conditioning but at its core is only pure love. And that's what your purpose is. To prove that only and only true love exists and in any form it should be respected. Rukmini is not someone else but a strand of your own energy to take care of Krishna *(Shiva)* as the ruler of the country."

Radha *(Shakti)* bowed to Lord Vishnu and repeated, "Love is love and nothing else." And Lord Vishnu left knowing he had taken care of Radha's *(Shakti)* doubts and helped her awaken again to her divine Love.

Nothing can come in between two people who love each other. Even if thoughts of separation are painful, the universe will send someone to help the Beloved remember their love once again. The Universe never allows you to give up on true love.

Shivshakti

Chapter 39

So much has to be understood about Shivshakti. It is a complex pattern of energy that keeps uniting and separating to unite once again at a higher frequency.

When Parvati was angry with Shiva for not responding the way she wanted him to and went to her father's palace to spend a few days, she got some insights. She just couldn't digest the fact that it was always she who told Shiva she couldn't live without him. He seemed to do very well without her. She always felt her pain at separation was more than his. She was angry at his inability or unwillingness to express his emotions. He always shrugged things off saying all was well. She was always wanting to hear words of love and longing and it would never be so. Shiva would never give in to her demand and would keep silent. His masculine aspect did not allow him to get vulnerable and open his heart fully.

Shakti was restlessly walking to and fro in the courtyard of her father's palace when Nandi came to visit her. She smilingly ran to greet him and asked, "Nandi, how are you? And how come you have come down from Kailasa to meet me? Is all ok up there? Is your Lord ok?" Nandi bowed down and said, 'Mother, I just came down to visit you as I am your son and was missing you. The abode seems empty without you, Mother. Father also seems restless and empty without you." Shakti immediately retorted, "Your father doesn't miss me Nandi, he never says so. He always seems fine with or without me."

Nandi shook his head from side to side and said, "Oh Mother! You are Jagatmata, how can you not see Father's pain, love and passion for you? He may not express it but hear his silence Mother, you will realize what all he hides and doesn't utter as he might not be the most expressive of his emotions. He carries 1*vish in his throat. He is Neelakantha. He keeps all the poison inside him Mother. So he speaks less lest he releases it out of his system and causes harm

1*Vish - Poison

to anyone, especially his shrishti. Mother he is in pain, without you, he cannot be happy and he keeps waiting for you to come back to your abode."

Tears welled up in Shakti's eyes and she was overwhelmed. Suddenly she could hear Shiva's silence which was singing the song of his soul's longing for her. It was their song, the soul song which belonged to them as lovers, as twins. It was the music of their love.

She ran in to pack and take leave of her parents to go back home with Nandi. She wanted to go back to her Beloved, back to her Shiva, back to their abode Kailasa where she belonged by the side of her Shiva.

SHIVSHAKTI

Chapter 40

Sati *(Shakti)* was sitting and crying, feeling no one understood her. She was in love with Shiva and no one could see why. Her family did not see Shiva as an ideal husband. Her father mocked Shiva's appearance and called him an [1]*Aghori*. He wanted a king like himself for his daughter. He did not see her love for Shiva. He loved his daughter from a materialistic space. He understood the language of money, success and luxury. He was so consumed by being a King that he could not see or understand a higher aspect of devotion. He didn't have any respect for a man who didn't wear rich ornaments, didn't ride horses or fought wars and conquer kingdoms. For him he worshipped Lord Vishnu who granted him the luxuries in his life. He failed to see his child's soul journey. His spiritual self was consumed by his ego self. His focus was always his kingdom, power and riches.

[1]*Aghori - A clan of tribal people

He had utter disregard for Shiva because of his attire, the snakes he carried on his body, the ashes he applied on his forehead and the rudrakshas he wore around his neck and hands. He found Shiva very bizarre as he didn't fit into the norms of society or the image of perfect groom for his daughter that he had in his mind. He was so obsessed with findings this perfect groom that he refused to see, feel and believe in his daughter's truth of her true love and did everything under his control to keep Shiva and her apart.

He kept punishing Sati *(Shakti)* and giving her arduous tasks so she could forget Shiva. But how could Sati *(Shakti)*, who felt Shiva in every cell of her from the day she saw him do so? Her knowingness was so strong that she couldn't take her mind off Shiva. She saw him everywhere, in the sky, in the sun, in the moon, in the trees and just could not forget him. If she tried hard, she could see him in her dreams.

He would speak to her as a Beloved in the dreams and they were so real that she would be distracted when she woke up and her urge to be with him would increase. She would be able to hear their song of their soul from his heart to her heart and knew that she just had to focus on reaching his abode in Kailasa. He was waiting for her.

There were times when she would be sidetracked from her truth but then every time she wanted to give up as she felt she was wrong in disobeying her father, the universe would not let her do so. She would get messages from the universe in many different ways to keep pursuing her goals and that was her truth and nothing else. Many a times she was caught in the conflict between her physical reality and her inner truth - the truth of her soul. She would call out "Shiva, Shiva, Shiva" and feel a sense of calmness and love overflowing from her heart to him. She would become ¹*magna*, taking his name like she was intoxicated.

¹*Magna - Go into a trance

Little did she know that Shiva the greatest masculine was waiting for her with the same impatience, but she had to pass many tests to reach there. Only then would love be recognized and cherished.

Love was to be tested so it could be clear that love was the only energy that exists in this universe. There is only one true language and that is the language of LOVE.

Chapter 41

Shiva and Shakti were sitting on their asana and chatting. Nandi, Ganesha, Kartikeya and others were running around and the sounds of laughter echoed in the mountains going down to the earth realm.

Just then Narad Muni came to visit them and bowed down to Shivshakti, who together were a complete feast for the eyes. He asked, "Pranam Ishwar and Ishwari, how is it that Maa can manifest herself on earth and in the lower realms and Shiva remains in the upper realm. Please explain."

Shiva smiles and answers, "Pranam Narada, I cannot permeate below a certain realm. I am the purusha, the entire sky and universe. Mata is prakriti, the whole sansara consists of her energies. So she is everywhere and can descend to a few lower realms. In every human also, Shiva resides only till the crown and cannot come down lower but Shakti operates as the Maa Kundalini in the roots. She doesn't allow humans to rest and stagnate. She keeps coaxing them to ascend and evolve. Shakti brings their energies to the level where they have to look within. It is the Devi who can be with the ¹*Bhu and sky. It is she who can be the Kundalini and reside within each cell of the human energy body."

Narad Muni then asked Shiva to explain Kundalini more fully. Shiva then continued, "Kundalini is a manifestation of Shakti hankering to meet Shiva in the crown. The desire of each human eventually is to merge their lower self with their higher self, to merge their divine feminine with their divine masculine. So Kundalini is Maa Shakti residing in everyone's root chakra urging them to rise up to merge. This whole process can take a minute or a lifetime depending on the individual. When Shakti begins to rise she has to pass through each and every chakra. When her energy begins to reach a particular chakra, the elements or issues around

¹*Bhu - Earth

that chakra begin to clear up. It is an opportunity to clear one's mind, karma, emotions. Shakti does a great service to humans by clearing the respective issues and karmic energies till she reaches the heart where she begins to overflow into the universe. As she rises up further in the throat, she begins to impart wisdom through that individual. It is a blessing to have a rising Kundalini. The process may be very tough but it is transformative and the rewards are very great. It is very important to understand the journey of Maa Kundalini within, which is akin to her journey spending 108 lives to finally become Shiva's Parvati. When the Kundalini has to pass through the throat to the third eye, the passage is very narrow and it is not an easy journey, but she crosses everything to reach the third eye to open up the senses beyond the five senses so one can experience the different dimensions that exist within and without. She finally reaches the crown to merge with her Shiva and the merger opens up the thousand-petalled violet lotus which can attract enormous grace from the Light. That individual would have by then cleared his major karmic journey. It is a great service Maa Shakti provides humans.

Narada feels overwhelmed listening to this entire energy display of the love of Shivshakti in person. He feels deep gratitude that he could understand and assimilate this truth.

Shivshakti is the ultimate truth of this universe. It resides in every cell of each and every living being and manifests in different ways. It makes sacred geometric patterns and creates mandalas of energy in every labyrinth of life that leads to Shambala.

Chapter 42

Shiva was strolling with Shakti in the meadows. His grandeur was very striking. He had the ability to move swiftly and effortlessly like a breeze passing by. He imparted magnificence to his surroundings even in his unusual attire. Shakti would look at him in awe. Wearing the simplest of clothing with flowers adorning her body, she was fragrant and fresh as an angel with wings spreading love and grace.

They were discussing the earth realm. Shiva explained to her that they had to manifest on the earth in special land spaces to keep transmitting the energies of Shivshakti so that the earth can keep breathing in its essence. That is why the twelve Jyotirlingams and many more plain lingams are located in the different grids of the earth to act as powerhouses for human beings to clear their karmic layers and absorb light.

Similarly, he explained, the 108 Shakti Peethas were to help humanity receive the grace of the mother for deriving strength and power. These powerhouses on earth are all interconnected deep under the surface to create brilliant light above as well as below. They create mandalas in the grid of the earth and are always spreading divine light. The entire solar system and the grid of the earth are interconnected and keep creating pillars of light needed for the transformation of the soul. The inner journey of the human soul is the very essence of Shivshakti and cannot be manifested in any other way. It is the balance of logic and intuition. The intricate patterns of the human body made with such precise perfection are only an example. It consists of minute cells creating sacred geometry which is continuously connected to the higher realms attracting Shivshakti. But the magnificence cannot be seen with the naked eye. Every living being palpitates on the same principle and thrives on the energy of the union.

When the illusions of the consciousness are cleared and vibrations rise to match the heavens, one can only breathe in the divine and nothing else.

Looking into Shakti's dove shaped hazel eyes, Shiva added, "Shakti, when humanity evolves, the sacred geometry evolves, the heavenly magnificence evolves and you and I evolve too. It is a continuous process of growth and ascension within me and within you and within this entire universe. That is when aging and maturing happens infinitely in the cosmos. What you and I are today, we were not millions of years back. We are also rising and growing in our consciousness along with the entire shrishti. You, Shakti, and I, Shiva, live forever in everything!"

Holding hands they walked through the forest in silence which too was evolving at a fast pace just like the rest of the universe. They knew they existed in everything and it was in a continuous continuum.

Chapter 43

Shakti and Shiva were once again deep in discussion about the earth and their own energies that permeated the entire [1]*Brahmhand*. These were intense powerful energies that helped the universe evolve.

Shakti asked Shiva, "Prannath, during our last discussion, you explained that you and I are constantly evolving and so are no longer the same as we were long ages ago. We have raised our vibrations very high, as compared to our earlier state. I want more clarity on this. Can you tangibly show me how we are different? Is it in the way we would respond to a situation? Every Yuga has its own way of handling situations. A man and a woman in every Yuga have acted from different principles. So if they existed now how would they be different? How would a Sati, Sita or a Radha be different from what they were in past? How would a Shiva or a Ram or Krishna be different now?"

[1]*Brahmhand - Universe

Shiva cleared his throat and said admiringly, "Shakti, what an intelligent question. First of all, the Shakti of thousands of years ago when we united wouldn't have asked any such question but you now have the ability to seek and use your masculine logic and intelligence at the same time. The Sati *(Shakti)* we know had the strength to stand up to her family and marry Shiva. But the less evolved feminine strand within her, made her feel shame and rage to such an extent that she jumped into the fire just to get back at her father who has insulted her husband by not inviting him to a grand *yagna*. The present-day Sati *(Shakti)* would not have reacted in such an extreme manner. She has evolved to a level of understanding where it is ok if people have different opinions. She doesn't keep her parents on a pedestal and will not allow their disapproval to upset her so badly. She would wait patiently and work on her relationship and hope that one day her father would see how happy she was with Shiva and embrace their love. She would know that her father's lack of acceptance was just her love being tested by the universe. She had no need to jump into the fire."

Shakti was very pleased to hear this and applauded loudly, her laughter rippling across the icy mountains. She asked "And what about Sita? How odd, I just noticed that their names have the same letters interchanged! Shiva smiled naughtily and said, "As if you don't know they are one and the same; their core essences are the same. The separation is only in human eyes not in those of the divine. Anyway, coming to Sita, the evolved Sita would know she is a king's daughter and a warrior. She would know how to protect herself. She would not need Laxman to look after her and draw a [1]*Laxmanrekha* and that's exactly why she forgot it was there. She got so caught up in the illusion as she was naïve. She herself is empowered to draw her own [2]*rekhas*. She would be in touch with her intuition and know that the illusion of the deer masked the reality of Ravana. She would be empowered to handle her life. And in case she made a mistake, she was yet empowered to stand up for

[1]*Laxmanrekha - Setting her boundaries
[2]*Rekhas - Boundaries

herself and not wait for a rescuer in Rama. She would have made sure she had the resources to leave when need be and no one could dare hold her prisoner like Ravana did. She would not have borne the atrocities of Ravana. Her self-worth and self-love would make her think of herself too along with others. She would have the ability to face any situation head on."

Shakti had a gleam in her eyes as she visualized every word Shiva was speaking. The sun was setting and it was suddenly dark and time to return to the abode.

They both turned around to walk back hand in hand, feeling safe with each other and comfortable with their own sexuality and personalities, unapologetically being who they were and setting an example for others.

Chapter 44

The sunrise was always a mesmerizing sight in Kailasa. Everyone who lived around Shivshakti went to the cliff to watch in awe the sun rising and the first rays of the sun falling on Kailasa imparting it their golden hue! They would all sigh together loudly in wonder. It was a pleasure to be around Shivshakti and watch them the first thing in the morning.

As they sat on their asana, Shakti asked Shiva to continue from where he had left off. Shiva was wondering where to start. There was so much to understand and discuss. It could last for eons. But he had to start somewhere so he began with Radha. Shiva knew Shakti was pretending ignorance so that he could, while explaining it to her, he was actually getting clarity himself. She being the Devi actually knew about all these great feminine energies as they had all emerged from her.

He nevertheless continued. "Let's talk about Radha. She was already in a much awakened state, as despite being married and having a household, she still loved Kanha to the level of devotion that someone can only have for her Beloved. She had a knowingness of her Beloved and felt no shame in professing her love for him. She was quite fearless to that extent. But somewhere their duties towards others came in between their love and she became the epitome of sacrifice once again. The duty of Rama and Krishna, in both their Yugas were towards their [1]*praja* but actually it came from the divine masculine choice to separate from and never be united with Sita and Radha. Their dedication to their Beloved is sung of even now in this Yuga. The feminine hadn't matured to a space where she had learnt to stand up for herself in front of the divine masculine. She was so in complete surrender to him that all that was expected from her was sacrifice for the larger good of all. She was asked and always expected to make sacrifices.

[1]*Praja - People of the kingdom

The evolved Radha and Sita would now make a stand and not allow false allegations of not being chaste against themselves. Their purity would be judged by their intentions and not their bodies. Their purity would be judged by their answering the call of their soul and not by the performance of their duties. A duty is karma bound and it should not be extended beyond that. It is not that one should not be doing one's duty but when to stop and where to draw a boundary and how to honor the soul's longing also needs to be understood. The new-age Sita and Radha would not be deterred by allegations and take false blame on themselves. They would not allow people's opinions to affect their self-image. They would make their own moral choices."

He further continued in one breathe, "If the masculine were to evolve enough to stand by his Beloved and not allow anyone to point a finger at her image or character, false allegations wouldn't matter. If he would not sacrifice his beloved just to honor his dharma to his praja, false allegations and blame wouldn't be allowed any play. If he would stand by her, he would provide an example to the people on how to behave with and honor the divine feminine. People pray to Shakti but that never deters them from questioning her moral values. This should not be permissible."

When Shiva finished talking, there was a loud silence which lasted for a whole minute. Both were stunned at the level of wisdom that had just poured out. Shiva knew it was Shakti's leela to make him aware of the divine masculine role in the ascension of the energies. He understood how much injustice had been done to the divine feminine for thousands of years. He bent his head down before Shakti asking for forgiveness for his actions of the past as a collective masculine energy and she accepted it and pardoned with grace and was joyous that the objective had been accomplished.

No longer would a male ever abandon his Beloved for his family, duties and other people's views. He was no longer that weak. He was the epitome of true strength and valour. He had now learnt to balance and discern between the truth and duties, between soul karma and personality karma. And thus, Shivshakti unites once again in all its glory and ascends to a higher level.

ANITA RAJANI

Chapter 45

This time Shakti was the one to ask Shiva, "Prannath, have you understood the role of Meera *(Shakti)* in Bhakti yoga?" Shiva murmured a "No" because somewhere deep within as he didn't have the guts to admit he didn't understand the concept fully yet. Shakti looked shrewdly at him and he immediately owned up and humbly asked Shakti, "Beloved, please explain. Sometimes my understanding of a concept may be different from yours as it is informed by the consciousness of the divine masculine while yours is by that of the divine feminine. So please go ahead and tell me."

Shakti showed him a vision of how Meera *(Shakti)* was born in human form and was brought in a very traditional household. Her worship of Krishna *(Shiva)* was her everything. She had one single focus and didn't have any other goal but to merge with Krishna *(Shiva)*. No one around her understood her Bhakti [1]*bhava* but that didn't deter her from her goal. She was forcefully married to a king

[1]*Bhava - Emotion

and life tempted her with all the material comforts but her goal was still and only Krishna *(Shiva)*. Meera *(Shakti)* was tested at many different levels in many different ways. Society was uncomfortable with her ways and tried to make her conform. But her soul purpose was to show humanity how Bhakti yoga can release you from your karmic body."

Shakti told Shiva, "Prannath, notice her single-minded devotion. See how her every cell vibrates to the name of her Lord. She has no proof he existed as her dimension of living on earth was different from the realm from which she came. Her existence was questioned by everyone around her. She was rebuked, punished, outcasted and even given poison to drink but her devotion was so pure and so complete that she was untouched by any of it. They couldn't intrude her mind and personality and shake her devotion. No one could harm her in any way. In fact the poison also became 2*amrut. Such was her level of devotion."

2*Amrut - Elixir

Shiva was listening intently and there was a loud silence after she finished. He then asked Shakti, "But would a new age evolved Shakti also approve of such devotion? Does it not run counter to her personality?"

Shakti laughed and replied, "Being evolved and ascended doesn't mean that Bhakti doesn't exist. Meera *(Shakti)* was so truly empowered that despite being a woman nothing deterred her or scared her. She was empowered and fearless and a true example of a divine feminine who once she has a goal can pursue it with complete fearlessness and strength. She should be applauded as a true Shakti because only Shakti can achieve this."

It's only Meera (Shakti) who could dive so deep into Bhakti of her Lord that nothing else mattered. It's a lesson learnt through Meera's persona, of how one-pointed devotion was a path to merger with the Lord.

SHIVSHAKTI

Chapter 46

Watching Shiva in meditation on his asana, Shakti's eyes went to the Ganga tied in his ¹*jata* and flowing from his head down towards Maa Dharti. Ganga said, "Pranam, dear sister? Why are you watching me so intensely?' Shakti then smiles at Maa Ganga and bowed to her older sister, saying and said, "Pranaam Didi, I wonder how you feel all tied up there. Do you feel suffocated or restless? Do you feel bound? Is it not an ²*anyaya* to you to be tied up like this? You are a divine feminine and it's the divine masculine who has tied you up. Do you want me to help you be released from my Prannath's jata?"

Ganga was silent for a moment. overwhelmed by Shakti's love and concern. She replied, "Dear Mata, you may be younger than me as I am the first born, but you are *Jagat Mata* - the mother of the universe - and I feel privileged by your concern. I am very happy here in Shiva's jata. Actually, I will explain. When I transformed

¹*Jata - Lock of hair
²*Anayaya - Injustice

from a king's daughter to a flowing river, it was my transition from the material world to the elemental kingdom. I became a river which will always be flowing and have a higher purpose - a soul purpose of washing away people's sins. When people bathe in me, their soul realizations will be immense. They will embark on a journey of forgiveness of others and self. They will seek moksha and self-realization. I have an enormous and never-ending purpose on the earth. I have to keep flowing endlessly, traveling a vast distance through various places to reach the ocean and merge with the light. It's an immensely powerful process and the transmission of energy through my river form is immense. There are times I lose my ground and flow haywire. I need someone to direct me and hold my boundaries. So Shiva has not bound me, he has been holding my space and my boundaries and not running haywire and floods the earth. He has kept me safe and secure. So Mother Shakti, I am not in a bad place. I am blessed to be with Shiva. Only Shiva can hold me and no one else."

Hearing this Shakti was so happy that her happiness flew around like small whirlwinds, creating laughter all around the mountains while Mother Ganga was feeling ecstatic in her glory of being with Shiva. Such was the truth hidden behind the mask of illusion. If you can see behind the illusion the truth has a shining face!! Hearing their joy, Shiva awakened from his meditations and asked Shakti, "I was hearing your conversation with Ganga. Did you really believe that I would hold Ganga in my jata without her permission? Whatever the illusion of maya may make it seem, the truth is that as the divine masculine, I, Shiva, will never misuse or wrong anyone. I am responsible and in complete awareness of the challenges of the divine masculine and I am always here to protect and support Ganga in her endeavors."

She was proud of Shiva that he had empowered Ganga in this way. Shakti went up to Shiva and hugged him. And their embrace created lightning across the skies - the united energy of love in its eternity.

ANITA RAJANI

SHIVSHAKTI

Chapter 47

Shiva was in his Tridev roopa and was conversing with his triple self. He was interacting with his counterparts and talking about the different aspects of the work they needed to do in the coming days. Narad Muni came at that moment to Kailasa and was enthralled to see this roopa of Shiva. He could easily see how he was all three - Brahma, Vishnu, Mahesh. It was as if he got separated into three parts and manifested himself in his three forms which had different energies to help run the [1]*shrishti*. Each had a completely different aspect to him and yet they were one.

Shiva is the destroyer and the protector, Vishnu is the preserver and giver of material prosperity and Brahma is the creator. Fascinating how different aspects actually emerged from one single energy - Shiva! Just like we have different personality traits and different multidimensional energies, all existing within us together - so similar and so diverse. What an insight this was for Narada!

[1]*Shrishti - Universe

And then as if to add to this enthralling sight, in walked Maa Shakti in her three forms - Kali, Mahalaxmi and Saraswati. The divine feminine was also one Shakti into three. And they entered the courtyard to meet the Tridevs. The Tridevis and Tridevs looked a magnificent sight to behold. It was as if there was magic all around and even with so much magic, the realities didn't diminish. Both coexisted and created this oneness and separation, a pull and a push as if everything coexisted as the universe - as a heartbeat.

Shakti has separated into Maa Kali the destroyer and the protector, Maa Mahalaxmi the giver of abundance and prosperity and Maa Saraswati the mother of knowledge and wisdom. So when Shiva destroys, Kali protects and Vishnu preserves what Mahalaxmi gives as abundance and whatever Brahma creates, Saraswati gives wisdom and knowledge to it. It is a perfect combination of Shivshakti even when they are in separation, each complementing the other. Definitely, the best permutation and combination that could ever be manifested in the universe! For a male there is always a female. For a yin there is always a yang and for every Shiva there is always a Shakti.

Every mandala and sacred geometry that exists within the micro consciousness and macro consciousness still vibrates with Shiva having an equal opposite Shakti - the Dark and the Light!!!

Chapter 48

Shiva and Shakti were enjoying the early morning sunshine. The sun was just rising, imparting the sky a reddish orange hue. There were birds awakening to the sun's rays, flying around chirping melodiously. It seemed as if the sun was spreading its light over everything, making it all alive again. Nature is so enigmatic and magical if you look at it intently.

Everything is in synchronicity and coexisting so harmoniously. It is only humans who sometimes because of the web cast by illusion forget they are also a part of the same nature - nothing more nothing less. Holding hands and walking, they circulated around Mansarovar Lake three times, energizing the lake with sweet water where humans can clear their karmic energies with a dip. The lake is a representation of purity at its best. Walking ahead just a little, they reached Rakshas Tal and began circulating around it three times.

Shakti asked Shiva, "Beloved, why have you created two lakes and why is the water in Mansarovar sweet and this Rakshas Tal salty? Is there a reason? The energies are so different although they exist right next to each other. Prannath, please tell me. I want to understand the secrets of this universe which are so mystic. It is as if we are looking at these magical waters, which are intended to purify souls? Is it so?"

As they continued their circulation around the lakes, Shiva explained, "Although they are next to each other, they have completely different properties. Rakshas Tal is salty and Mansarovar is sweet. This is because we live in a multidimensional universe which has different kinds of souls inhabiting it. When human souls and divine souls reach here to purify themselves, they take a dip in Mansarovar Lake. It cleanses their minds and karma and lightens their souls. They need sweet water to make their mind and heart very calm. And when Rakshasas reach here to purify their souls, they take dip in Rakshas Tal. It can cleanse their negative properties for their souls to rise to the human level. They are the ones who need salty water to cleanse the extreme negative darkness of their souls. So the two are separate but again if you look intently they are a form of you and me as only your essence in the Kali roopa can purify such dark elements in Rakshas Tal while my intense energies as Kailaspati *(Shiva)* can purify humans in Mansarovar Lake. These lakes are also a form of Shivahakti at its best.

They both laughed and ended their circulations and headed back to their abode to Ganesha and Kartikeya who were waiting to get their fullest attention.

SHIVSHAKTI

Chapter 49

Shakti began with a statement, "Brahma and Saraswati are very little spoken of!! Everyone just knows them as the creator and the Goddess of knowledge. Very few actually tap into these energies and pray to them. In fact, it is forbidden to have temples to Brahma on the earth and the Saraswati River also disappears as she is stated to have been cursed. Why so Prannath? What is the reason behind this?"

Shiva smiles and says, "Shakti you know the essence of Brahma *(Shiva)* is to create. I created him so he can create the world. The work assigned to him is to help create positive and negative charges in the world in accordance to its needs. He cannot do so without his counterpart Maa Saraswati's *(Shakti)* knowledge, expertise and wisdom. Take for an example a production factory. The designs and the knowledge of the machines is imparted by one and another person or a unit merely creates the products and hands over the creator. Both are very important. None can do without the other. But there is a huge caveat here. Mere knowledge and the ability to create like a magician can create ego and thus destruction. It is imperative that they both stay grounded and balanced at all times so when they are needed they can provide the best of creations to the universe. Brahma *(Shiva)* and Saraswati *(Shakti)* were both condemned for their ego as it very easy to develop ego when you have knowledge."

Shakti was staring wide-eyed at Shiva and said, "That's fascinating! I have never understood this aspect before." Shiva replied, "I haven't finished yet. Hear me out fully. Every creator on the earth is like an artist. A designer or a builder needs to imbibe the knowledge of Saraswati and creative abilities of Brahma. Only then can they create the best creations and deliver at their best but they also need to be detached. Both Brahma *(Shiva)* and Saraswati *(Shakti)* have been forbidden too much exposure since if any human imbibes their energies, they can develop ego and become akin to the Ravana and would need to be beheaded like him. It is important to be humble and have the wisdom of knowledge rather than ego of the intellect".

Shakti observed the sky turning orange with the setting sun creating an illusion of the sky glowing like fire. She remarked, "Knowledge also needs a stable ground else it can create illusionary perspectives of self and make a monster of anyone. I understand now why Saraswati *(Shakti)* was cursed by Ganesha and went invisible. She needed to learn the lesson of turning her knowledge into wisdom. She is remarkable in her grace and if it falls upon anyone he can embody the brahman within him and become a creator of magic."

Truly astonishing how Shivshakti manage to become different parts to role play different games to keep the universe running. And at the same time they were in a constant continuous continuum!!

ANITA RAJANI

SHIVSHAKTI

Chapter 50

Narad Muni was spending some time with Shiva learning, growing and integrating new learning. At one point he asked Shiva, "Deva, why are people in the world not happy. Why are they suffering? How can they be relieved of their pain and suffering? Pray tell me. The people are caught in the web of ¹*maya*. They are full of illusionary desires, needs, lacks and voids. They are running after things they might not get or fulfill them the way they think it will. They are not even aware of their goals or soul purpose. Why do you send them down with so many veils and distractions? What kind of game is this? Is it fair to them? If they are all a part of you then why are you covering them in the veil of suffering? What's the real reason? Pray explain."

Shiva was smearing ²*bhasma* on his body and drawing his trikon tika on his forehead. He replied, "The earth itself is an illusion. Do you know Narada why do I wear bhasma? It's a reminder that

¹*Maya - Illusion
²*Bhasma - Ashes

everything is eventually destroyed and then recreated. Nothing is permanent. Everything is moving constantly in the universe vibrating at different frequencies and creating different permutations and combinations. Do you know Narada why I draw these three lines on my forehead? It is a reminder that the past, present and future are all in the mind. It is a reminder that time is linear and we are living all at once. There is no past or future. It is all in the here and now! It is also a reminder that anything in states of three is stronger than anything else. Do you know Narada why I carry Vasuki, the snake around me?

Patting Vasuki Shiva continued, "He is a reminder that we should not give in to our worst fears and should always lead life fearlessly. Even something as dangerous as a snake with a poisonous bite can be overcome. What more do you want to know? The veils are there but lots of clues around the truth lead those who seek it. Despite the clues all around, people blindly follow superstitious beliefs. The darkness that precedes them takes over. The game of life is created by me, so consciousness can evolve and Shivshakti can keep transcending time and space and rise above the dimensions and expand the cosmos. Every particle consists of me. When humanity removes the veils and begins to see Shivshakti within and without, they merge into me and attain 3**moksha*. Their game is over. They no longer carry any ancestral curse or need rebirth or family or children. They attain the highest level of growth in temporal life and come back to me. It is designed so I learn and grow and evolve. It is a game of raising consciousness. The planets and the thousands of suns and moons that exist are all a part of Shakti and me. We are the creators and we are the destroyers. We are the game and we are the game changers. When each person can attain Shivshakti within them only them can I attain the final embodiment of the actual strength of my light. I am Shivshakti."

3*Moksha - Enlightenment

Instantly he took the form of Ardhanarishwara. It was a sight whose magnificence is equal o a thousand suns shining together. And suddenly it became so clear that Shiva existed within Shakti as Shakti existed within Shiva. There was no other place they could exist. Paripoorna as they seemed to be in total embodiment of love that expressed itself fully. *Shivshakti* is nothing but love radiating throughout the universe as one energy, one heart.

Narad Muni bowed down to this magnificent sight of love and light and understood that all humanity needed to do was embody Shivshakti within them to unfold its highest potential as a soul to get moksha. It was so simple yet so profound!

Chapter 51

Shakti was sitting lost in her own thoughts, completely at peace and in bliss when Shiva came by, and said something so judgmental that it put her in a rage.

She started wondering what her fault was. She was just sitting down doing her own thing, she was not even engaged with anybody, she was not talking or chatting, neither was her attention on Shiva, then why? Why did Shiva do this to her? What was that made Shiva always want to break her trance of happiness, her determination to be her own strength. This time, in spite of all the wisdom and understanding of everything telling her not to react and always be quiet. All the wisdom she had that told her if one is angry; in spite of knowing that relationships need to work on adjustments, she chose to break all these beliefs and all this conditioning and ask Shiva, Why?"

She walked across to him He was wearing a mask of ego, wanting to attack her because he couldn't take her strength, her persistence, love energy. He couldn't understand how somebody could so love. His ego, his pride, his mask would not allow him to see himself that way. He turned defensive when she said to him, "Shiva, I need to ask you something.' He became offensive in defense and told her angrily, "I do not want to talk to you." She had not done anything and had only said, "Shiva, Can I ask you something?" but he went into a rage about how incompetent she was and that she was not good enough. She just stood there rooted to the ground, not understanding, why he was behaving in that way. What had she done? She could think of nothing which made him to react in such a way. But yet there he was, reacting.

She went away completely thrown off balance and, angry. She sat down near Mansarovar Lake, staring into the water. A beautiful, pure, powerful lake and when she looked into it, she saw her own reflection. It was so beautiful, so magnificent and so powerful. She looked at that image and said, "Why? Why is he seeing something so bad and being so judgmental about me?" In that moment her own reflection, the Shakti in the lake, said to the Shakti looking down at her, "'He couldn't take your unconditional love, how expansive you are, He couldn't take how strong you are in all circumstances and before all challenges. He couldn't accept that even in your silence you are a very very powerful Shakti."

Shakti sat deep in thought staring at her own reflection wondering "Why? He is Shiva, he is the most powerful man., Why is he thinking like this? Why am I a threat to the so magnificent, Jagat Pita Parmatma? Why should I be a threat to him?" She sat there in silence, but she was very sure of one thing, come what may, she was not going to budge from her strength., She was going to retain her power even if the one who she loved the most, had shaken her up in a way she would not have allowed anyone else to shake her. For that matter, Shakti would have destroyed any other energy that would have shaken her up this way. But he was Shiva, her

Shiva, the one she loved the most, and she was his ¹*Ardhangini, his other half. He was her mirror."

Just as she sat in that silence, thoughts tumultuously chasing each other in her mind, yet strong and perfectly poised, she saw Shiva walking towards her, She straightened up a bit, about to get defensive but catching herself said, "No, I am not going to get defensive, I am going to see, watch, observe calmly, I am going to watch him, what he wants to say, as a calm, detached observer." And as she watched him with his long strides, walking toward her, her love for him about to overflow ready to forget everything in one instant. But she did not react, she waited and watched him coming closer and he came and stood by her.

She stood up in her complete strength and Shiva told her "Shakti, I am sorry, I shouldn't have behaved in that manner with you." Shakti did not reply, she did not budge, she chose to be the observer and Shiva continued, "Shakti, when I see you so magnificent, when I see you so powerful, when I see you facing

¹*Ardhangini - The better half

challenges so beautifully without getting shaken, which I can't, when I see you with so much strength, and I know you are Shakti for a reason, I would do anything to be in your place., But I am not Shakti. I am Shiva and as Shiva I am not that powerful without you. But you know Shakti, you are very powerful even without me and that threatens me, that thought, feeling, how you can love me so much, so unconditionally? How can you be my strength so beautifully? I cannot be as powerful as I would love to be without you, because without you I am nothing. You are the Shakti energy, you are the energy running through my veins, and if you don't exist, I don't exist. But you will always exist even without me., That is what threatens me and I chose ignorance when you came to me., I chose my ego when you came to me, but when I saw you retaining your power and balance in spite of that, it hit me very hard and my ego got shattered in that moment and I realized how powerful you were and how magnificent you were. I bow down to you my Shakti, and I would always love you to remain so powerful

ANITA RAJANI

without feeling threatened. I will take care not to feel threatened by your strength, because I have realized it is only my ego that is hindering my own growth and as that is gone I am one level further evolved Shiva who has now acknowledged his Shakti as she is."

In the eternal dance of Shivshakti, they came together once again in one moment of union before the dance began anew. The pull and the push would continue as always and these unions would create, blooms of energies sent to the universe to create something magnificent and beautiful.

Chapter 52

Ganesha and Kartikeya were playing in the aangan of Kailasa, the abode of the ideal family of Shivshakti. They were laughing, giggling and running around. The sounds of the laughter of the children were echoing in the universe like fresh creativity spilling around for people to channel. Getting tired they flopped to the ground, on the beautiful white snow, giggling and giggling, looking up at the beautiful white skies which looked like Angels spreading their wings and blessing them. The sunshine gleamed in their little childlike eyes, both embodiments of the eternal, magical child.

Kartikeya suddenly turned to Ganesha and asks him, "Ganesha, do you remember that time when Father told us that whoever would go around the world three times and come back first would be the winner?" Ganesha nodded his head and said, "Yes brother, I remember.Why are you asking?" Kartikeya went into a series of thoughts and intense thinking suddenly asked Ganesha another question, "Why do you think I lost? I did go around the world three times and you did not. You just circumambulated mother and father and they voted you the winner. They said that a parent is equivalent to the whole universe, but I am not able to understand or intellectualize the concept. Did you understand it? Can you explain it to me?"

Ganesha smiled at Kartikeya and sitting up turned towards Kartikeya and said, "Brother, I will explain. There is a reason why I chose to go around mother and father rather than going around the entire universe." Kartikeya also sat up and looked very interested. Ganesha explained, "Brother, understand Shiva and Shakti - Mother God and Father God - are a representation of this entire universe." Kartikeya jumped in and asked, "But how?"

Ganesha replied: "Wait, let me explain, have patience Brother. Every cell every atom, every molecule of this entire universe is made up of the divine feminine and divine masculine. They all are a part of our Mother God and Father God. The entire universe has been conceptualised on this idea of the masculine and feminine vibrating equally together that denotes creation. Every creation that you see on this earth, in the universe and the galaxy, the Sun has a moon, the stars, the blue vast sky, everything is made up of tiny particles of Shiva and Shakti, our father and mother, yes our father and mother. Similarly, when male and female humans come together and give birth to a child, they are the representations of Mother God and Father God, as they are representing the actual Mother God and Father God and creating new beings on the earth, a new creation."

Ganesha continued, "So now, have you understood, why going around father and mother was actually the way to win. It was a task given by the father to see which one of us understood this concept better than the other. It was a test for us. It was to make us realize, that beneath everything, beneath everything that you see, everything that is conceived in this universe, every creation that exists in this Universe that has existed before and that which is yet to come into existence is based on the energy of Shiva and Shakti. That is the actual root of each and every manifestation of creation. And they must be respected at all times in all aspects."

Kartikey went silent, absorbing this knowledge and trying to understand and grasp what was being said and he bowed down to Ganesha and said, "Brother, I'm so glad that at least you could understand this concept and explain it to me. I am so proud of you, my brother, that you are so intelligent." Ganesha simpered and told him, "I am also a part of their creation brother and so are you. How will we not know what this is all about? It was just a matter of looking within to find the answer, because there are no answers outside and all the answers lie within."

Kartikey got the message loud and clear and understood that whenever the universe/Father God/Mother God/ ShivShakti tests us, we should not be running around to look for the answers. The answers lie within us as we are a part of their creation or we ourselves are a creation which has branched out of Shivshakti itself. So how can any answers be outside of us?

Chapter 53

Shiva and Maa Shakti were doing their eternal dance - the tandava - in their abode of Kailasa. They were surrounded by all the Devas and Devis watching them, mesmerized by the energy, grace, power they both exuded through the dance. The dance seemed a game of a push and pull and yet was in perfect synchronicity with each other. They seemed to be so lost in each other enjoying their love that they were oblivious to the divine beings around them. For them there were just the two of them, everyone and everything else stopped existing. As if time had stopped and they existed in some realm where the two were merging with each other in totality. This sight was a magical moment for all. So they had gathered here to watch them.

While watching the Shivshakti dancing in the most enigmatic dance ever seen, Maa Laxmi told Maa Saraswati, "This dance is so mesmerizing. Doesn't it exist in all living forms. Isn't this dance is what is creating duality?" Maa Sarawasati, spoke with utmost wisdom, her eyes still locked on the dance, "This is exactly what creates the duality my dear. It's the pull and push in all human emotions, day and night, ebb and flow of the sea, dawn and dusk, hot and cold, summer and winter. It is the good and bad and the up and down. It is the in and out and also the within and without. It is the dark and light. It's the laughter and the crying. It is the being loved and being unloved. It is the - me and you. It is as above so below. It is the infinite abundance and poverty. It is the [1]*dukha* and *sukha*. That is what this dance represents: everything that's moving in perfect synchronicity in the universe creating opposite forces to coexist with each other as complementary forces, not co-dependent but interdependent. Their dance is all about the minute changes within us taking place in every cell

---

[1]*Dukha and Sukha - Sadness and Happiness

which dies every day and is reborn into new cells every day. It is what keeps this universe alive. This Tandava is interwoven across the universe. Devi Laxmi, you have understood this correctly. This is so mesmerizing that we rush here to watch it every time it happens. We evolve watching it just as they evolve dancing it."

The music that was filling up the entire cosmos, the sounds of their payals and the thumping of their heartbeats was also singing its own song. The bodies were only energy flowing in and out of each other. Wide eyed Laxmi and Saraswati and all the other divine beings continued to watch fascinatedly the divinity that was being created in every moment of the Tandava. They didn't want to miss any of it.

Just watching them magically dancing creating the ebb and flow of the universe, the movements of the world and the cosmos. Shivshakti were entwining themselves within each other more and more each time they danced creating more oneness in the universe and dispelling the darkness which co-existed to create the wonderful shrishti. Truly they are the ultimate energy growing and creating new dimensions within their own energies challenging themselves at all times.

Shiva and Shakti Dancing in deep Bhakti

Of love so divine

like yours and mine!

Energies entwining

Merging and uniting,

Creating a new love

As white and pure as a Dove!

It's my only way to mukti

to take me on with ride of bhakti

for we are meant to be

till eternity together shall we be!!

ANITA RAJANI

SHIVSHAKTI

Shiva! Oh Shiva!

You are our Jiva

Sitting on a rock

Your eyes closed and manes in locks

Your trishula and your dumroo

Your weapons to release our junoon

Wearing a rudraksha as your ornament

Ashes on your body is your patent

Doing the eternal dance of tandava

You make our hearts sing new ragas

Oh Shiva! Our blessed father

Bless you children and see they don't falter!

ANITA RAJANI

You Write. We Publish.

To publish your own book, contact us.

We publish poetry collections,

short story collections, novellas and novels.

contact@thewriteorder.com

Instagram- thewriteorder

www.facebook.com/thewriteorder

www.ingramcontent.com/pod-product-compliance
Lightning Source LLC
LaVergne TN
LVHW041915070526
838199LV00051BA/2619